THE SISTERS
GRIMM

8

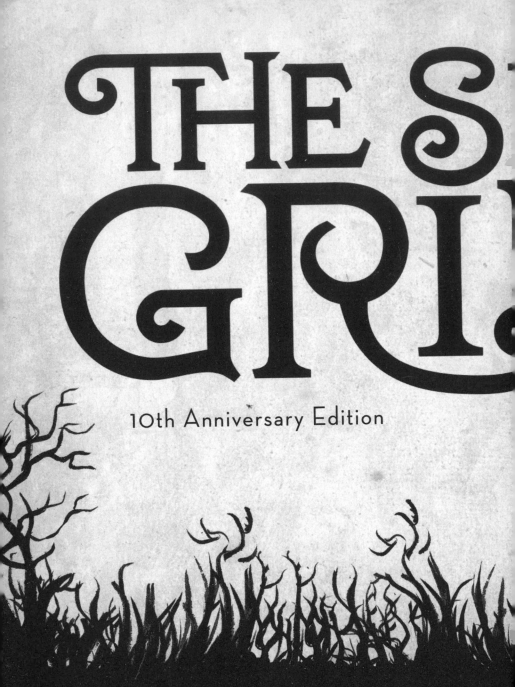

THE S

GRI

10th Anniversary Edition

THE INSIDE STORY

MICHAEL BUCKLEY

Pictures by PETER FERGUSON

AMULET BOOKS   NEW YORK

Cataloging-in-Publication Data has been applied for and can be obtained from the Library of Congress.

ISBN 978-1-4197-2006-2

Originally published in hardcover by Amulet Books in 2010
Text copyright © 2010, 2018 Michael Buckley
Illustrations copyright © 2010 Peter Ferguson
Book design by Siobhàn Gallagher

Printed and bound in U.S.A.
10 9 8 7 6 5 4 3 2 1

Amulet Books are available at special discounts when purchased in quantity for premiums and promotions as well as fundraising or educational use. Special editions can also be created to specification. For details, contact specialsales@abramsbooks.com or the address below.

ABRAMS The Art of Books
195 Broadway, New York, NY 10007
abramsbooks.com

For two very good editors,
Susan Van Metre and Maggie Lehrman

Y ou have ruined everything!" Granny Relda shrieked, sparks crackling from her fingertips.

Energy blasted from her hands and shocked Prince Charming. While he was distracted, she grabbed his sword, then thrust it into his side. Charming fell over and moved no more.

Suddenly, the world shook with an explosion so violent that it sent Sabrina falling to the ground. Before she could stand, there was a second explosion. The noise rattled her eardrums, and the hot wind scorched her face, neck, and hands. But the third explosion was the most frightening. The earth fissured and cracked, releasing a skin-searing steam from below. It wasn't a mist or a fog—it was alive, made from something old and angry.

"This is not good!" Daphne shouted over the din. "We have to stop it!"

"Be my guest!" Sabrina cried. What was she going to do against magic that powerful? She wasn't an Everafter. Still, this wasn't her first near-death experience. She had always managed to find a solution in the past. Where were all her brilliant ideas now?

There was a fourth and final explosion, and the steam morphed into a single form. It solidified into a creature with eyes like bottomless pits and a smile that froze Sabrina's bones.

He was free.

1

Three Days Earlier

(Or Half an Hour...
It's All in How You Look at It)

I DON'T THINK WE'RE IN FERRYPORT LANDING anymore," Sabrina said to her sister, Daphne, slamming the front door shut. She leaned against it and took in her surroundings. The small farmhouse was rustic, with a dirt floor and shabby furniture—three chairs, a rickety table, two tiny beds, and an iron stove. To call it a house was generous. It was more like a shack, but it was also a prison for the time being. The sisters Grimm were trapped inside. They were completely surrounded.

"They're singing for us," Daphne said, looking outside.

"Get away from the window," Sabrina scolded.

Daphne giggled and bit down on the palm of her hand. It was a quirky habit that came out when she was very excited or very happy. "We're here. We're actually here!" she squealed.

Sabrina pushed a chair against the door to keep it closed, then joined her sister at the window. Like their surroundings, Daphne had changed. Gone were her overalls and sneakers. Instead, she wore a yellow dress. She smiled brightly, her eyes filled with curiosity as she peered outside. There, the girls found hundreds of little faces staring back at them.

They watched as a very short, chubby old woman dressed all in white stepped through the crowd. Three men accompanied her, each with a bushy white beard and untamed eyebrows. They wore matching blue suits and pie tin–shaped hats. No one in this group or in the gathering throng was more than three feet tall. The woman stepped up to the front door and knocked.

"We *are* here, aren't we?" Daphne exclaimed with a delighted squeal. "We're in OZ!"

Sabrina studied the road leading away from the house. It was paved with yellow bricks.

There was another knock on the door.

"This is so awesome!" Daphne cried.

"No, Daphne, it's not awesome. Everyone from Oz is crazy!" Sabrina snapped.

"That's not a very nice thing to say. They're just unusual. I can't believe we're here—or, I guess, we're technically only in the story about Oz. I didn't believe it was possible when Mirror told us about the Book of Everafter, but look! We're inside a real live fairy tale!"

Sabrina bristled at the mention of Mirror, and a wave of sadness swept over her. Her throat tightened, and she fought back tears. She felt betrayed, heartbroken, and confused. She never wanted to hear Mirror's name again.

"I wonder when Dorothy will show up," Daphne mused as she stepped back from the window.

"Try to focus," Sabrina insisted. "We jumped into this book to save our baby brother. We don't have time to waste on some idiot from Kansas. We need to come up with a plan."

"Maybe we should start with opening the door?"

There was another knock, this one quite a bit more urgent than the last.

Sabrina ignored it. She sat down on one of the creaky beds. "They can wait. I . . . I really don't know what to do."

"I'm sorry," Daphne said, "but did the great Sabrina Grimm just say she didn't have a plan?"

Sabrina knew her sister was teasing, but she couldn't crack a smile. She was completely at a loss for ideas. She and Daphne knew next to nothing about the Book of Everafter, and the new territory made Sabrina's head spin. How did it work? What were the rules? Could they be injured while they were inside—or, worse, killed? They had a hard enough time staying alive in the real world. How could they survive in a magical book? And there was Pinocchio to consider. Where was he? Was he still a threat? And Puck! He'd stepped into the book at the same time as the girls, but he was nowhere to be found. Was he lost? Injured? Dead? Should she and Daphne go looking for him or wait here for him to show up? There were too many questions with no answers! Trying to understand all of it made Sabrina feel nauseated. Her heart raced, and she had trouble catching her breath. What if she made the wrong decision?

"Well, we can't just sit here all day. Maybe the Munchkins have seen Mirror and Sammy. They could point us in the right direction," Daphne urged.

"Who is Sammy?" Sabrina asked.

"Our baby brother," Daphne explained. "I can't just call him 'what's-his-name' forever, so I'm calling him Sammy, unless you can think of something better. I'm open to suggestions. Anyway, we should get going."

Daphne opened the farmhouse door. The three men and the little old lady were waiting for them. They smiled brightly. "Welcome—" the woman started, but Sabrina slammed the door in her face.

"We can't just barrel into this without thinking," she snapped.

"It could be dangerous. If the Book of Everafter really does have every fairy tale ever told, then it's filled with some really nasty stuff. You know as well as I do that some fairy tales are full of monsters and murderers."

"So we'll kick butt and take names like we always do," the little girl said matter-of-factly, assuming the karate stance she'd learned in Snow White's self-defense class. Then she opened the door again. The old lady and her friends were waiting, looking confused.

"Welcome—" the woman started hopefully, only to have Sabrina slam the door in her face again.

"This isn't the real world, Daphne. Just take one look around, and you can see something is off. Everything is too bright and too cheery, and too many things are the exact same color—like the sun and the flowers outside and your dress. They're all the same shade of yellow. The Munchkins outside look weird, too, like they're slightly out of focus."

"Big deal! I don't think we need to be afraid of the color yellow or some blurry Munchkins," Daphne said.

"What I'm trying to say, if you'll just listen, is that we can't assume things work here like they do back home. This book has its own rules. Like that dress you're wearing—you didn't have that on when we jumped into these pages. Where did it come from?"

Daphne looked down at the yellow dress. "Why did it change my clothes and leave you alone?"

Sabrina was still wearing her jeans, sneakers, and sweater. "It's weird."

"Well, big sister, Granny Relda says the only way to solve a mystery is to jump right in." Daphne pointed to the door. "And you don't seem to have any better ideas!"

Sabrina groaned. "Fine! But stay close. And just so you know, I have no problem serving up a plate of knuckle sandwiches to these weirdos!"

"Be nice," Daphne insisted as she opened the door once more.

"Welcome!" the old lady said quickly, bracing herself for the door.

"Hi!" Daphne said.

The crowd of Munchkins in the square gaped in wonder and let out a collective "Oooohhhhhhhh!"

The woman in white cleared her throat and bowed as low as her old bones would allow. "You are welcome, most noble Sorceress, to the land of the Munchkins. We are so grateful to you for—"

"No problem," Sabrina interrupted, rolling her eyes at Daphne. "So, we're looking for a man traveling with a little boy. Has anyone seen them?"

The Munchkins seemed startled by her response.

"You are welcome, most noble Sorceress, to the land of the Munchkins. We are so grateful to you for having killed the Wicked

Witch of the East and for setting our people free from bondage," the old woman recited again.

"I told you, they're nuts!" Sabrina growled.

"Wait a minute! We killed who?" Daphne shouted. She pushed through the crowd, grabbing Sabrina's hand and dragging her along. The duo found a pair of feet wearing silver shoes sticking out from under the farmhouse.

"Oh, no!" Sabrina cried.

"Someone call nine-one-one!" Daphne shouted. She knelt next to the feet. "Lady? Are you OK? I'm sorry we dropped a house on you."

"There is nothing to be done," the old woman said in an irritating, singsong voice. "She was the Wicked Witch of the East, as I said . . . She has held all the Munchkins in bondage for many years, making them slave to her night and day. Now they are all set free and are grateful for the favor."

Daphne ignored her and shouted at the feet again. "We've called for help. We'll get you out of there soon. Does it hurt?"

One of the tiny men stepped forward. "Child, that's not the line. Are you attempting to alter the story?"

Sabrina and Daphne shared a confused glance. "Huh?"

The woman in white leaned in close and whispered, "That's not what you are supposed to say. You have to ask me if I'm a Munchkin."

Sabrina scowled and clenched her fists. "Can we save the stupid games for later? There's a woman trapped under this house, and—"

"Wait!" Daphne interrupted, turning to the woman. "Are you telling us we have to say the lines from the story? Why?"

One of the men stepped forward and whispered, "If you don't, you'll attract the Editor."

"And the Editor is bad?" Daphne whispered back.

The man nodded. "Very bad."

"OK, we'll try. Are you a Munchkin?"

The woman sighed with great relief and smoothed some wrinkles out of her dress. "No, but I am their friend. When they saw the Wicked Witch of the East was dead, the Munchkins sent a swift messenger to me, and I came at once. I am the Witch of the North."

"Wrong! Glinda is the Witch of the North," Sabrina sneered.

Daphne shook her head. "That's in the movie. Glinda's the Witch of the South. Haven't you read the book?"

"I skimmed it," Sabrina admitted. "Sorry, but all the weirdos we've met from Oz have kind of ruined the whole story for me."

Another of the little men chimed in quietly. "No, you're supposed to say, 'Oh, gracious! Are you a real witch?'"

Sabrina stamped her foot and fumed. She didn't understand the game the Munchkins were trying to play with her and

Daphne, or why they had to play it at all. "Just let me punch one of them," she begged her sister. "It will be a lesson for the others."

"Silence your animal, Dorothy!" another Munchkin snapped at Daphne. "She's going to get us all into trouble."

"Did you just call me an animal?" Sabrina growled.

"Dorothy?" Daphne said. "My name's not—wait! You think I'm Dorothy?"

The Munchkin nodded. "You were assigned the role when you entered the tale, and you must play along. If you change the story, there will be grave consequences for us all!"

A happy smile spread across the little girl's face. "I'm Dorothy! That explains the dress."

"Dorothy's dress is blue," Sabrina argued.

"Nope, that's the movie," Daphne said.

"Whatever. If you're Dorothy, then who did the book turn me into?" Sabrina asked, looking down at herself for some clue.

Daphne snickered and pointed to Sabrina's neck. "You're not going to like the answer."

Sabrina found she was wearing a small leather collar. She pulled it off and studied the silver tag. The name TOTO was engraved in the metal. She threw it to the ground in anger. "Of course! I have to be the dog!"

Daphne laughed so hard, she snorted.

"Keep laughing," Sabrina fumed. "Just don't be surprised if I bite you."

Another of the little old men stepped forward. "Please, we beg you. Just say the line."

Sabrina threw up her hands in frustration. "I feel like I'm trapped in a second-grade play. We don't have this story memorized. They're going to have to spoon-feed us every line of dialogue."

"We'll just have to do our best," Daphne said. "'Oh, gracious! Are you a real witch?'"

"Yes, indeed," the woman in white croaked. "But I am a good witch, and the people love me. I am not as powerful as the Wicked Witch who ruled here, or I should have set the people free myself."

"Great!" Sabrina cried. "Now, we'd love to stand around all day learning this book word for word, but we're sort of dealing with an emergency. We're looking for a man traveling with a little boy. Have you seen them or not?"

"He's short and balding and wearing a black suit," Daphne added.

A rosy-cheeked Munchkin in the back of the crowd made his way to the front. "I have seen him," he announced.

"Mirror was here? Are you sure?" Sabrina pressed.

The rest of the Munchkins broke into agitated complaints, begging their friend to be quiet and not change the story. He refused. "It's best to just get them out of here as quickly as possible. They're ble. They're just like the last fellow. He wouldn't follow the rules, either," he said, then turned back to the girls. "We didn't ask his name. We just wanted him to go, so we sent him down the Yellow Brick Road to the magic door."

"Magic door?" Daphne asked, raising her eyebrows.

"They pop up at the end of a story. Never seen one myself, but I've heard rumors. Apparently, they take you into another story."

"We have to stop him. If he gets to the door, who knows where he'll end up next?" Sabrina said.

"How do we find this magic door?" Daphne asked the Munchkin.

"The best way to find it is to follow the story to its end," the witch said. "Follow the Yellow Brick Road, find your companions, and meet the great and terrible Wizard. He'll send you to collect the broom of the Wicked Witch of the West. Kill her, then return to the Emerald City. Once all that's done, the door should appear."

"That will take forever," Sabrina complained.

"Isn't there another way?" Daphne asked.

The witch shook her head. "Honestly, you'll never make it. You're deviating from the story so much that you're sure to attract the Editor. I'm surprised he isn't here already."

"Who is this Editor?" Daphne asked.

Everyone shushed her at once. "Don't say his name! He'll hear you!"

"You're afraid of him?" Sabrina asked.

They all nodded.

"If you're smart, you will be, too," the good witch said. "Now, we've already said enough. Please, just leave us and don't come back."

Sabrina rolled her eyes. "Happy to, lady! C'mon, Daphne, if we're ever going to get to the end of this story, we have to get going."

Daphne nodded. "OK, but what about Puck?"

Sabrina shrugged. "I'm hoping we'll find him along the way. Right now, we can't waste any more time."

"Well, nice to meet you all," Daphne called to the crowd. "Sorry we killed that witch."

With that, the girls headed down the Yellow Brick Road. They didn't get far before they were stopped in their tracks by angry shouts. When they spun around, the girls found a Munchkin with a red face and a long beard chasing them. He repeatedly tripped over his beard as he ran. He handed Daphne the silver slippers that the Wicked Witch of the East had been wearing.

"You forgot these," he gasped, catching his breath. "They're a big part of this story, you know."

"Thanks," Daphne said sheepishly.

"Oh, and one more word of advice—stay inside the margins," he said softly.

"The margins?"

"Don't wander into parts of the stories that weren't written down," he whispered. "Dangerous things live there."

Before Daphne could thank him for the advice, he turned and stomped back up the Yellow Brick Road, muttering something about "story wreckers."

"He was pleasant," Sabrina grumbled.

"C'mon, Toto," Daphne said with a wink. "We've got a bad guy to catch and a little brother to rescue. Be a good dog, and I'll rub your belly later."

"Keep it up, and I swear I'll dig a hole and bury you in it," Sabrina snapped.

"Bad dog!" Daphne teased, grinning. "No treats for you!"

The countryside of Oz was very strange. Ancient trees lined the roads, each covered in knots and cracks that looked like withered faces. Birds with strangely colored plumage flew overhead. One sported feathers with a black-and-white checkered pattern. It landed in their path and eyed them curiously before returning to the air.

Each bend in the road revealed a strange new animal or a field of peculiar flowers. Sabrina enjoyed the light breeze. It had a warm scent like fresh oatmeal cookies or vanilla. It helped to calm her nerves and made their mission more bearable.

They walked on the Yellow Brick Road for the better part of a day, keeping their eyes peeled for signs of Mirror and the baby. They found no clues and wondered if Mirror had taken the child off the path to hide in the woods. Sabrina didn't know much about the Land of Oz, but she knew it was big. Mirror and the baby could be anywhere.

At sunset, Sabrina and Daphne finally stumbled across their first sign of intelligent life—a family of Munchkins living in a round blue house. The father, named Boq, invited them inside for dinner. The girls were famished and exhausted, but they declined. Daphne explained that they were trying to rescue their baby brother, but Boq and his family were intent on sticking to the original story. They argued that Dorothy and Toto were supposed to eat and stay the night with them, but the girls refused. Boq chased them down the road for a mile and a half, begging them to return. Eventually, he gave up and walked back the way he had come, defeated.

"They're really freaked out about this Editor dude," Daphne commented. "But I've never heard of him before now."

"He must be from one of the later Oz books," Sabrina said. "Baum wrote fourteen of them. I wouldn't worry too much. Even if we do run into this Editor guy, I'm sure we can take him."

By dark, the girls were ravenous. They shook the limbs of the next fruit tree they found. Apples and oranges fell from above, as well as many bizarre fruits Sabrina had never seen. Daphne happily munched on them all, but Sabrina stuck to the familiar ones.

"I wasn't sure we could eat these," Daphne said between bites. "I thought maybe they weren't real."

"It's like we're walking through a painting or something," Sabrina said.

"Or like we're in someone's memories of Oz and not the real place," Daphne said.

Sabrina nodded. Daphne's explanation was spot-on. Everything was a little bit fuzzy and incomplete.

The girls ate until their bellies were full, and then they lay down under the tree and gazed up at the unfamiliar constellations in Oz's now-dark sky.

"I'm worried about Puck," Daphne said.

Sabrina was, too, but she grunted dismissively. She didn't want her sister to know how concerned she was about the boy fairy.

"I keep having this terrible thought," Daphne continued. "If the Book turned me into Dorothy and you into Toto, what if it turned Puck into that dead witch back in Munchkinland?"

"That wasn't him. We would have recognized his stink. Even a dead witch's corpse smells better than Puck. If we're lucky, that was Pinocchio sticking out from under the house."

Daphne groaned. "I can't believe he was working with the Master. I mean, Mirror. I mean . . . whoever."

"I used to be so good at judging people," Sabrina said. "At the orphanage, I knew exactly who we could trust and who we couldn't. Now, it seems like every time I turn around, someone we thought was our friend is conspiring against us."

Daphne slid her hand into Sabrina's. It helped unravel the knot of worry in Sabrina's belly a little.

"We've got each other. That never changes," Daphne reassured her. "And Mom and Dad, and Granny and Mr. Canis and Red and Uncle Jake. You can trust them. And baby Buddy."

"Buddy?"

"Sammy didn't feel right," Daphne explained. "Remember Sammy from the orphanage?"

"Soggy Sammy Cartwright," Sabrina said with a grimace. "He always wet the bed."

"Buddy sounds better," Daphne declared. "I wonder what Mirror calls him."

Sabrina's heart sank. "I doubt Mirror calls him anything at all. He doesn't see our brother as a person. Just a body he wants to steal."

"That's sad. Everyone needs a name."

Sabrina chuckled. "I wouldn't get too used to 'Buddy.' Mom and Dad probably have some ideas of their own. I think one of the perks of having kids is getting to name them."

Daphne sighed. "You're right."

A moment later, the little girl was sleeping deeply, her snores drifting high into the tree's branches. Sabrina closed her eyes but couldn't sleep. Her baby brother's face kept flashing in her mind— his red hair, his big round cheeks, his beautiful green eyes. But it was impossible to imagine his innocent little face without Mirror's wicked one appearing, as well.

How could she have been so wrong about him? And, worse, what else was she wrong about?

The next morning, the girls woke achy and stiff from sleeping on the ground, but there was no time to complain. They collected more fruit from the tree, shoving as much as they could into their pockets for later. Daphne found a stream, and the girls drank greedily and washed their faces. Soon enough, they were off again down the Yellow Brick Road.

"We've been in this story for a whole day," Sabrina pointed out as the rising sun blinded her. "Everyone back home is going to freak out. They have no idea where we are."

"You forget that we come from a very smart family," Daphne said. "I wouldn't be surprised if we ran into them before we get to the Emerald City."

Sabrina shook her head. "I'm not sure smarts matter much when it comes to this place. We jumped into the Book, but it seems pretty random where it placed us."

"Mirror's in Oz, too," Daphne reminded her.

"Yeah, but Puck and Pinocchio aren't," Sabrina argued. "Even if our family figures out what happened to us, they might land in a different story and never find us. I hate to say it, but I think it would be best if they just stayed where they are. The last thing we need is for our whole family to be completely lost in a bunch of fairy tales."

"Well, our family isn't exactly known for sitting things out."

"That's what I'm afraid of." Sabrina sighed.

They walked for hours before coming across a farm with a picket fence. Not far from the road, mounted on a tall pole, was a scarecrow—*the* Scarecrow, who served as the librarian back in Ferryport Landing. They recognized the friendly face painted on his old burlap sack and the goofy blue hat he wore. Sabrina now noticed that it matched the ones the Munchkins in the square had been wearing.

"Good day," the Scarecrow said, lifting his head to speak to them.

"Just ignore him," Sabrina muttered, trying to usher her sister along. She suspected this storybook version of the Scarecrow was just as much of an idiot as the real-life one. The last thing the girls needed was a clumsy, chattering moron slowing them down.

Daphne stopped. "Sabrina, we can't just ignore him."

"Oh, yes, we can," Sabrina said. "He's a walking disaster. I still have a lump on my head from the last time he dropped a stack of books on us."

"You heard the Munchkins. We have to follow the story to find the magic door, and he's supposed to come with us."

The Scarecrow looked confused. "You're supposed to say—"

"Shut up!" Sabrina cut him off.

The Scarecrow's painted eyes grew wide with astonishment. "Would you help me down?" he asked shyly.

"Absolutely not!"

Daphne frowned and stepped closer to the fence. "I'm sorry, Mr. Scarecrow, but we can't. We're trying to rescue our brother, and you, well, how can I put this—"

"You're a royal pain in the behind," Sabrina finished.

"You dirty little fleabag!" the Scarecrow snapped back at Sabrina. He squirmed and struggled, but he couldn't free himself from his post.

Sabrina took her sister by the hand and pulled her down the road. "Sorry, but you're on your own, Scarecrow. Good luck!"

"Wait!" he cried. "I didn't mean it."

"Sorry!" Daphne cried.

"But you need me for the rest of the story," the Scarecrow called.

Sabrina ignored him. She was determined to put as much distance as she could between them and the Scarecrow as quickly as possible. His desperate cries continued for another few minutes before he fell silent.

"That was mean," Daphne grumbled.

"Daphne, he's not real. This whole world and everyone in it is just magic. It's a spell."

Her little sister crossed her arms with a huff and marched along in silence. The sisters didn't speak to each other for the rest of the afternoon.

The farmlands of Oz soon faded into a thick forest. After only a few minutes in the dense wood, Sabrina heard a loud groan from within the trees.

"Did you hear that?" Daphne asked, spinning around frantically to look for the source of the cry.

Sabrina rolled her eyes. She knew the story well enough to know where the noise was coming from. "Keep walking. It's the Tin Man."

Daphne bit down on her palm. "The Tin Man is my favorite! We have to rescue him!"

"Don't even think about it." Sabrina shook her head. "If we left the Scarecrow, we can leave this guy, too."

Daphne ignored her and raced off into the woods.

"Daphne, no!" Sabrina chased after her, and soon the two girls came upon a cabin. Standing nearby was the Tin Man, rusted stiff with his ax in hand. He mumbled something unintelligible, but Daphne didn't stop to listen. She raced into the cabin and reappeared with an oilcan in her hand. She poured black grease into the Tin Man's joints, and soon he was moving about freely, if a bit awkwardly. Daphne finished the deed with a healthy squeeze of oil into his jaw sockets.

"I might have stood there forever if you had not come along," the Tin Man said. "So you have saved my life—wait . . . something's missing. Where's the Scarecrow?"

The girls shared a look.

"Back on that pole," Daphne admitted, her face burning red with embarrassment.

"You left him?" the Tin Man cried.

"Yep," Sabrina said matter-of-factly, grabbing her sister by the hand and pulling her down the road. "So you should consider yourself lucky, pal. See you around!"

The Tin Man followed them. "Uh, h-how did you come to be here?" he sputtered.

"We're going to see the Wizard so we can kill the Wicked Witch," Daphne said.

The Tin Man stopped in his tracks. "That's not what you're supposed to say."

"We're doing things a little differently," Sabrina said.

"Come on, Tin Man. Come with us," Daphne pleaded.

The Tin Man reeled back on his metal heels. "Uh, you know, I don't really feel comfortable with this."

"Then, don't let us keep you," Sabrina called over her shoulder.

"I didn't even get an autograph," Daphne complained.

"He would slow us down," Sabrina said, though in truth she was relieved she wasn't going to have to hang out with a talking garbage can.

Daphne scowled and continued onward.

With every step, the forest encroached farther on the Yellow Brick Road. Soon, the girls found themselves beneath a canopy of limbs and leaves so thick that it blocked the sun. Sabrina felt a sort of surreal déjà vu. She suddenly understood what was about to happen.

"The Cowardly Lion is coming," she said, looking around.

"I wish we got some kind of warning," Daphne groaned. "I haven't used the bathroom in a while. If he jumps out and scares us, I'm going to wet my—"

Before she could finish, a monstrous beast hurled itself out of the trees. It was a lion, but a much bigger one than Sabrina expected. Nearly as large as an SUV, he had huge muscles and paws as big as tennis rackets. His black claws gleamed like daggers, and he looked ready to devour the two of them. But his ferocious face quickly turned to confusion.

"Where are the others?" he growled.

Daphne attempted to answer but only let out a little whine.

"Who do you think you are?" Sabrina cried. "You just leaped out of nowhere, roaring and acting all crazy! Now you've made my sister wet herself!"

"No, I didn't," Daphne muttered.

The Lion furrowed his brow and let out a roar so powerful, it blew the girls' hair back.

"But that's not helping," Daphne continued.

"I . . . I don't know how this works without the others," the Lion said. "Let's just keep going. You have to hit me in the face."

Daphne shook her head. "I can't hit a lion in the face."

The Lion roared again, then leaned in close and whispered, "You have to. It's part of the story."

Daphne looked troubled. "Sabrina, I can't do it."

"Fine. I've got this," Sabrina said. She wound up and punched the beast square in the nose. He went down like a sack of potatoes and lay unconscious on the ground.

"It was supposed to be a tap!" Daphne cried.

"How is it my fault that a lion as big as a tank can't take a punch from a twelve-year-old girl?" Sabrina asked, rolling her eyes. "C'mon, let's keep moving."

"We can't just leave him here in the middle of the road," Daphne said. "Can we?"

"You want to carry him?" Sabrina asked.

Daphne looked down at the massive beast and sighed. A moment later, she stepped over the lion to join Sabrina, and together they continued down the Yellow Brick Road.

"Have you noticed how scared everyone gets when we don't

follow the story?" Daphne asked. "The Lion looked like he was going to lose it when we didn't show up with the Scarecrow and the Tin Man. This Editor person must be a really bad dude."

Sabrina shrugged. "People don't like change. Remember how panicked Uncle Jake was when the Butcher, the Baker, and the Candlestick Maker changed the jelly in their doughnuts from raspberry to blueber—Wait, what is this?!"

The girls had come upon some kind of sinkhole in the Yellow Brick Road. It was a gaping pit that seemed to go on for miles in both directions, and there was no way to walk around it. Sabrina peered over the edge but couldn't see its bottom.

"That's one big pothole," Daphne muttered.

"You would think that a city made out of emeralds could find the money to fix the roads," Sabrina said. "You've read this story. What did Dorothy do to get across?"

"She used us," a voice said from behind them. The girls spun around and found the Scarecrow, the Tin Man, and the Cowardly Lion approaching. They all looked very angry.

"You two are causing mayhem all over this story," said the Tin Man. "You can't just abandon major characters by the side of the road."

"Or in the middle of it," the Cowardly Lion growled.

"We happen to be very important parts of this story," the Scarecrow said, as if his pride were as bruised as the Lion's nose. "You can't get through it without our help."

"And if you keep making changes, the Editor will revise us all."

"OK, who is the Editor?" Sabrina demanded.

"Hush!" the Cowardly Lion cried in a panic. "He'll hear you!"

"What is so scary about this Editor person?" Daphne asked.

The Cowardly Lion lowered his voice to a whisper. "He guards the Book of Everafter, ensuring the stories collected in its pages remain untouched. He will not tolerate any adjustments. Please, stop changing the story."

Daphne turned to Sabrina. "Maybe we should do what they want. I have no idea who the Editor is or what story he's from. He could be dangerous."

Sabrina sighed. "Fine! It doesn't matter anyway. We're stuck here on the wrong side of this massive hole!"

"Lion, put Dorothy and Toto on your back and jump across this ditch. When they're safe, come back and get the rest of us," Scarecrow instructed.

The Tin Man and Scarecrow helped the girls onto the Lion's back, and with one great leap, the creature jumped to the other side of the sinkhole. Sabrina and Daphne tumbled off his back and watched him jump back across to retrieve the others.

"OK, now I've wet myself," Daphne said.

"Me too," Sabrina admitted.

The sinkhole proved to be only the first in a long series of obstacles.

There was another ravine to cross—this one guarded by creatures with the bodies of bears and the heads of tigers. The monsters followed the sisters and their traveling companions onto a log they used to cross the gap, but Sabrina shoved the makeshift bridge over the edge, sending the creatures to their deaths below.

Then came a raging river where the Scarecrow insisted he get stuck on a pole halfway across because it followed the original story. Sabrina and Daphne tried to talk him out of it to save time, but the Oz characters felt it crucial to stick to Baum's tale.

"I know the Scarecrow is hoping the Wizard gives him a brain," Sabrina complained, "but I think the Cowardly Lion and Tin Man need new ones, too."

Sabrina did her best to be patient, but when they arrived at a massive poppy field, she lost it. She remembered the flowers from the movie and knew that anyone who stopped in the field would fall asleep and eventually die.

"This is just insane!" Sabrina cried. "The Yellow Brick Road is the only way to get to the biggest city in Oz, but it's riddled with giant holes, vicious animals, and now these stupid deadly flowers!"

The Oz characters looked just as exhausted as the sisters Grimm. "Toto and Dorothy, ride on the Cowardly Lion's back for as far as he can go," the Scarecrow instructed. "Then the Tin Man and I will come along and rescue you. Then, we'll meet the Queen of the Field Mice, who—"

"Queen of the Field Mice?" Sabrina said. "There's no Queen of the Field Mice!"

"Yes, she's in the book," Daphne corrected.

"Well, forget it!" Sabrina shouted. "We're trying to rescue our brother from a lunatic bent on stealing his body. And all of this is taking too much time."

The Tin Man gasped. "But the Editor will—"

"If you bring up your stupid Editor one more time, I'm going to melt you down and make you into hubcaps," Sabrina threatened. "We're done with this stupid story."

Sabrina stormed off to a nearby tree and sat down. Daphne followed and stood over her.

"So what do you want to do?" Daphne asked.

Sabrina looked out over the sea of poppies, desperate for an idea, any idea. But once again, she came up with nothing. She felt like she was trapped in a maze with no exits.

"I'll think of something," she promised, even though she wasn't sure it was true.

Daphne sat down and took off the witch's silver slippers. She'd been wearing them since Munchkinland. She rubbed her tired toes for a moment and then let out a scream that startled Sabrina.

"Um, duh," Daphne said, slipping the shoes back on her feet. "Why didn't we think of this before?"

"What?" Sabrina asked, confused.

"I guess I thought they weren't real 'cause we're in a book," Daphne continued. "But the fruit was real and those monsters seemed pretty real. If all that's real, couldn't the shoes be, too?"

The shoes!

"We can use Dorothy's slippers to teleport to the end of the story. We can skip all the dumb stuff and go right to the door. We could corner Mirror when he and the baby arrive," Sabrina cried, jumping to her feet. "Daphne, you're a genius."

"Absolutely not!" the Scarecrow exclaimed as he stumbled over to join them.

"That is not what happens!" the Cowardly Lion called. He was practically sobbing.

"Why do you care?" Daphne asked. "We're only skipping some stuff that doesn't matter."

"Doesn't matter?" the Tin Man said. "It all matters!"

Sabrina brushed herself off and pulled Daphne to her feet. She looked the others square in the eyes. "All that matters is finding our brother. This train is leaving the station. Are you coming with us or not?"

"But—" the Scarecrow cried.

"Daphne, start the chant."

"I really must object," the Lion roared.

Just then, a strange pink creature scurried out of the poppies. It was the size and shape of a watermelon. It didn't have eyes or a nose, at least not that Sabrina could see, but its wide mouth was filled with pointed teeth. A long, snakelike tongue shot out and licked the air. Sabrina made a mental note to stop skimming the books in the family library and actually read them from cover to cover from now on. This thing was definitely not in the movie.

"Revisers!" the Scarecrow cried.

"The Editor knows you've changed the story. He's come to erase us all," cried the Tin Man, his steely expression melting into fear.

"Erase us?" Sabrina asked.

From the poppies came a flood of the pink creatures. Hundreds of them spilled out over one another, all rushing toward the group.

"Get us out of here now!" the Cowardly Lion shouted, and the three characters rushed to stand arm in arm in paw with the sisters.

Daphne clicked her heels together and repeated three times, "There's no place like the end of the story."

There was a sound like a balloon inflating, and the world twisted into a knot before Sabrina's eyes. She remembered using the magic slippers in Ferryport Landing, but this time was much more turbulent. She felt herself shaking and spinning violently, out of control, until everything went black. A moment later, Sabrina staggered dizzily into the light, and a room came into focus.

Sabrina found that she and the others were now in a circular room draped in green curtains and decorated with dazzling emeralds. A throne sat high on a pedestal across the room, and a bright light shone from the ceiling.

"This isn't the end of the story," Sabrina said, looking around for the magic door.

"We're in the Wizard's castle," the Cowardly Lion whispered, clearly afraid of their new setting.

"I don't get it. Where's the magic door to get us out of this story?" Daphne asked.

"The door doesn't exist yet. It will appear when the tale is over," the Tin Man explained.

A roaring green flame burst to life in the center of the throne. Inside the flame hovered a massive head with sharp features and little eyes.

"I am Oz, the Great and Terrible!" the head bellowed. "Who are you and why do you seek me?"

The Tin Man, the Scarecrow, and the Cowardly Lion fell over themselves in fear. But Sabrina knew better than to be afraid. She might have only skimmed the story, but everyone knew the spooky floating head was only an illusion created by Oscar Diggs. He was known as the Wizard, or simply Oz, but he wasn't really a wizard. He created sophisticated machines that fooled the citizens of the country he ruled.

"We're looking for our baby brother," Sabrina announced. "He was kidnapped, and we're trying to rescue him. To do that we have to kill the Wicked Witch and get her broom for you, so why don't you do your little magic show so we can get on with it?"

The head opened its mouth wide. Sabrina expected more complaints about respecting the plot, but instead Oz let out a deep, obnoxious belch.

The girls looked at each another in disbelief. "I know that's not in the story," Daphne said.

The head laughed. "Why would I help a couple of monkey-faced freaks like you two?"

Sabrina glanced around the room suspiciously. Not far from where they were standing, she spotted a tall green screen. As she stepped toward it, the head shook in protest.

"Never mind the man behind the screen!" Oz bellowed as Sabrina dragged the screen aside. Behind it was a very familiar shaggy-haired boy in a filthy green hoodie.

"Puck!" the girls cried.

On the floor next to him, tied up with rope, was the Wizard. A green gag was shoved in his mouth, and it was clear that he was not happy. Puck, however, looked as amused as Sabrina had ever seen him.

"Hello, Grimms," he said. "Are you having as much fun as I am?"

2

"HOW DID YOU GET HERE?" SABRINA ASKED.

"When I jumped into that crazy book, I landed inside a tornado. It spun me around and around at a million miles an hour and flung me all the way to the Emerald City. It was awesome!"

Daphne looked down at the Wizard. His hands were bound tightly. "Is this your doing?"

Puck nodded enthusiastically. "His guards found me trespassing on castle grounds and locked me in a cell. Once he figured out I was from the real world, he let me out and begged me to help him escape the Book."

"Escape the Book? Oh, dear," the Tin Man murmured.

"Is that possible?" Sabrina asked.

"I highly doubt it," the Scarecrow said.

"Well, the Wiz thinks it is," Puck said. "I agreed to help, but

I've known Oz pretty much forever. I knew he would double-cross me as soon as he got the chance. So I thought I'd triple-cross him."

"Triple-cross him?" Sabrina asked.

"Yeah, it's double-crossing a double-crosser. But I was afraid he'd be too clever for that, so I went ahead and skipped the triple, quadruple, quindruple, sexdruple, and septdruple, and went straight to the octdruple-cross. He never saw it coming!" Puck cheered. "So, marshmallow, where'd the dress come from?"

"The book turned me into Dorothy," Daphne explained.

"What about you?" Puck asked, turning to Sabrina.

Sabrina's face turned bright red. "I'm Toto," she mumbled.

"Who?"

"I'm the dog," she snapped.

Puck exploded into an obnoxious, horsey laugh.

"Laugh it up, stinkface," she growled.

"Well, we've got a big problem, Grimm," Puck teased. "I can't marry a dog."

Sabrina seethed. "What are you talking about?"

"Our wedding, duh!" Puck said. "We're engaged."

It took several moments for Puck's words to sink in. Once they did, Sabrina was sure she'd misheard him.

"We're married in the future, right?" Puck continued. "I'll admit, I wasn't happy when you first told me. The whole thing made me sick. I mean, really physically ill. I was barfing and feverish.

I spent a few days in bed with the chills, until I realized getting married might be the best thing that ever happened to me! I'll have a servant to wait on me hand and foot. You can rub my back and pick the bugs out of my hair and wash my underwear. I sure hope you can cook, Grimm. Because I love to eat."

"A servant?!" Sabrina cried. "That's what a wife is to you?"

"Of course," Puck said matter-of-factly. "We need to start the planning right away. What do you think about a destination wedding? Pompeii would be great, you know, 'cause of all those people killed by the volcano—nothing says romance like a dead body encased in volcanic ash."

"You've lost your mind!" Sabrina exclaimed, feeling a bit volcanic herself.

Daphne stepped between them. "We can talk about this later. Right now, we need you to fly us to the Wicked Witch of the West's castle. We have to get her broom."

"'Cause you're trying to finish the story," Puck said. "I get it. The Wizard told me a bunch about how this book works. Grab on tight and we'll be there in a flash."

"Stop! STOP! STOP!!!!!!!" the Tin Man shouted. "You people don't understand what you're doing. You can't just skip ahead. Lots of stuff happens on the way to the Witch's castle. The Editor won't tolerate such a dramatic change to the story!"

"Are they worried about this Editor person, too?" Puck asked.

"The Wizard was whining about him before I gagged him. I don't understand what the big deal is about this guy. Personally, if I was going to terrorize people, I'd come up with a better name than the Editor."

"True, there's nothing scary about the name Editor," Daphne said.

"Stop saying his name!" the Cowardly Lion groaned. "Do you want him to send revisers here, too?"

Sabrina shuddered, thinking about the grotesque pink monsters that had attacked them at the poppy field.

"Let's ditch the weirdos," Puck said, extending his wings to their fullest width.

"Absolutely," Sabrina said.

Puck took each girl by the hand, and soon the trio was flying away, to the sound of continued protests from the Tin Man, the Scarecrow, and the Lion.

"Honestly, I'm glad we don't have to witness what happens to them now," Daphne said. "The Scarecrow has his hay yanked out, the Cowardly Lion is chained up in a yard, and the Tin Man is thrown out a window of the castle."

"Really?" Puck said as they soared higher and higher. "Are you sure you want to miss all that? It sounds hilarious!"

Sabrina shook her head. "I want to get out of this story as quickly as possible."

Moments later, they were flying high over the spiraling green towers of the Emerald City. To the west, Sabrina could see nearly every part of the Land of Oz. Each region was wildly different than the last.

Puck flew on for hours until a menacing castle came into view. It was so dark, it seemed to be made out of shadows.

"That must be it!" Sabrina said.

Puck circled the castle in search of an entrance until he finally spotted an open window in a high tower. He swooped inside and landed, setting the girls down on a cold stone floor. The walls were covered in tapestries the color of the night sky. In a far corner, a dark figure hovered over a glowing crystal ball. She had black, unkempt hair, pale green skin, and a patch over her left eye. She was covered in warts, and her teeth appeared to be pointed—filed down into fangs like a shark's.

The arrival of the three children tore her attention away from the crystal ball. But instead of attacking them, the witch let out a startled yelp and backed into the corner.

"You're early!" she cried. "I'm supposed to send all manner of torment against you before you get here. You missed the flying monkey attack! And the swarm of killer bees!"

"Sorry to disappoint," Sabrina said, "but we're trying to move things along. Where do you keep the buckets of water?"

"Right, right," the Witch muttered. Shaking off her confusion, she rushed across the room and fetched a bucket full of hot, soapy water. She placed it in front of Daphne and whispered, "Maybe the Editor won't even notice the change. In this scene, you are scrubbing the floors. I'll go out and come back in, and I'll be very angry. All you have to do is throw the water on me. Then, I'll melt."

The Witch raced out into the hall.

"I don't want her to melt. I'll have nightmares," Daphne whined.

"She's not real, Daphne," Sabrina said.

The Witch raced back into the room with a wicked expression on her face. It quickly morphed into disappointment. "Why aren't you scrubbing the floor?"

"I'm not sure I can do this," Daphne said. "I don't want to murder you."

"But that's what happens in the story," the Witch argued. "Don't worry about me! I've done it so many times, it doesn't even hurt that much anymore."

Daphne frowned.

Puck snatched the bucket from the little girl. "I'll do it. I would love to see her melt."

Daphne snatched the bucket back. "No one is melting today!"

"I have to. C'mon, melt me!" the Witch begged.

"I never understood this part of the story, to be honest," Daphne admitted. "Does all water make you melt? How do you drink anything? What happens when it rains?"

"Is this really that important? Throw the bucket at me," the Witch pleaded.

"OK, everyone calm down," Sabrina said.

"Should I go back out and we can take it from the top?" the Witch asked.

"No! " Daphne said.

"Daphne, we can't get to the magic door unless she dies," Sabrina said.

"I know that!" the little girl cried.

"Here, I'll make this easy for everyone. Give me the bucket," the Witch said, trying to pull it from Daphne. "I'll pour the water on myself."

"No!"

"Kid, let go," the Witch demanded. "I want to melt! Really, I do!"

"You don't know what you want," Daphne snapped.

The Witch gave a mighty tug, and Daphne lost her grip. Water splashed across the Witch's body, and a low, hissing sound filled the room. The children could do nothing but watch as she began to dribble onto the floor like an ice cream cone on a hot day.

"Thank you sooooo much!" the Witch cried just before the smile on her face slipped down her dress.

"I said it before and I'll say it again: Oz rules!" Puck cried.

Daphne's face took on a green hue that rivaled the Witch's complexion. "I am never going to get over this," she grumbled.

"Well, would you look at that?" Puck pointed across the room.

A red door with a brass knocker had materialized out of thin air. Sabrina clasped the knob and pulled the door open. She was met with a blast of warm wind and the smell of a burning fireplace.

"So this takes us to the next story?" Puck shouted over the wind.

Sabrina nodded.

"Where do you think it's going to take us?" Daphne asked.

"Hopefully somewhere less annoying than Oz," Sabrina said.

"Like someplace where people don't melt," Daphne muttered.

Together, the trio stepped through the door. There was a whooshing sound as the floor dropped out from beneath them. Sabrina's stomach plummeted, but they soon landed hard on their feet.

They found themselves in some kind of somber library. Tightly packed books, some that looked as old as time, were arranged neatly on bookshelves soaring hundreds of feet into the air. A yellowing globe sat in one corner, and the head of some horrible alien animal was mounted above a crackling fireplace. In the center of the room was a high-backed leather chair, and sitting there was a thin, elderly man with hair as white as snow. A pair of spectacles sat precariously on the tip of his long, pointy nose. He leafed through a book with one hand and patted the head of one of the strange pink creatures with the other.

"What story is this?" Daphne whispered to her sister.

Sabrina checked to see if she had a new outfit, but everyone was wearing their own clothing. Even the silver slippers that had been on her sister's feet just moments ago were gone. Dorothy's shoes were resting in the man's lap. He placed them in the mouth of the pink monster next to his chair.

"Reinsert these into the story," he commanded. The monster backed away, and the man turned his attention to the children.

"I know the fairy: Puck, Trickster King, Imp," the old man said, gesturing to him. Then he turned his tiny eyes toward the girls. "But you two I do not know."

"We're Sabrina and Daphne Grimm," Sabrina said. "Who are you?"

"I am called the Editor," he said. "Did you say your last name was Grimm?"

Sabrina nodded.

Four more of the pink creatures crawled out from beneath the Editor's chair. He scratched affectionately at their grotesque heads and bellies.

"Am I to understand that the three of you are from the real world?" he continued.

Sabrina nodded again.

"I'll have you know, you've made a complete mess of *The Wonderful Wizard of Oz*. You butchered the dialogue, skipped over crucial plot points, and changed the climax. Right now, everyone reading this story finds a scene where the Witch begs Dorothy to kill her. If I can't fix it quickly enough, it will stay that way. Your mischief may very well have changed history," he said, and then rose from his chair. He crossed the room with his pet monsters following at his heels, then paused at the red door the children had just used. He knelt down to speak to the revisers.

"I'm afraid *The Wonderful Wizard of Oz* needs a complete rewrite. We're going to start over with this one."

The revisers squeaked eagerly in return. One licked the Editor's hand with its long white tongue, and then, to Sabrina's amazement, it split into five equal parts that grew rapidly into five completely new revisers. The other creatures did the same until there were twenty, then one hundred, and on and on and on. When there were so many they were pushing against the walls of the library, the Editor opened the door, and the whole herd lurched through the portal, their huge, fanged mouths open wide.

"How, exactly, do those things fix the stories?" Sabrina asked.

"They're going to erase everything so I can rebuild it."

"Erase?"

"I suppose 'eat' would be a more accurate word."

"Wait! Does that mean the people, too?" Daphne asked.

The Editor nodded.

"Can I watch?" Puck asked.

"You can't punish them for what we did," Daphne cried.

"That's what a reviser does," the Editor said. "They revise—the setting, the story, and the characters. When they are finished, I can re-craft the tale so that it matches the original account. You seem troubled."

"Duh!" Daphne snapped.

"If I allow you to make changes to the story, it could alter your world, too. Dorothy might be trapped in Oz for good. The Wizard would continue to rule the Emerald City through fear and intimidation. The Munchkins could be stuck living under the evil hand of the Wicked Witch of the East. Certainly you wouldn't want any of that to become reality, would you?"

"We just want our brother back," Sabrina said. "We're not here to cause trouble."

The Editor sighed impatiently. "It's just like a Grimm to play with forces you do not understand. Although, to be fair, you and your family aren't the only ones known to meddle around in this book."

"Well, this book lets you change your life. It's a little tempting to have it just lying around," Sabrina said.

"Yes, I see your point. But that is not what this book was meant to be. A hundred years ago, the Book of Everafter was created as a simple cure for homesickness."

"Homesickness?" Daphne asked. "I don't understand what you're saying at all, buddy."

"The Everafters left their homes to come to America. It wasn't an easy decision, and many of them regretted it, especially after the barrier was constructed around Ferryport Landing. To help ease their sorrows, the Book of Everafter was created to act as a living, breathing copy of the places and events cherished most by fairy-tale folk."

"You're saying this crazy place is like a vacation back home for Everafters?" Sabrina asked.

"It was. Its purpose has been altered dramatically, but at the time the pages were a chance for a person to visit old haunts and run into long-lost friends—or, rather, versions of those places and people. The early visitors to the Book said they found it comforting."

"But now it's different?" Puck asked.

The Editor sat back down in his chair. "A powerful sorceress altered the magic that fuels this place. She changed it into something it was never meant to be."

"And what's that?" Daphne asked.

"Please stop interrupting," the Editor snapped. "The sorceress warped the Book into something dangerous. Now, when someone steps inside, they can alter the stories, and those changes can become reality in your world. For example, let's say a princess decides that the man of her dreams is not so dreamy anymore. She can come into the Book and make it so that she never met him. When she returns to the real world, their lives together will have never happened. Any number of things can be altered, from keeping a princess from kissing a frog to stopping the Big Bad Wolf from eating dear, sweet grandmama."

"Sounds like a handy thing to have around this town," Puck commented.

"On the contrary, it is a terribly dangerous thing to have around. Why do you think the Grimms locked it up so tight? The changes have unpredictable consequences. The sorceress who changed her own story learned that the hard way. She caused chaos in nearly every tale and even changed me. I was created to be a sort of tour guide, someone who could help Everafters find their stories, but after the witch wreaked her havoc, I became the guardian of these stories. The revisers help me keep things from getting out of control, and for some time now, we've enjoyed a bit of peace and quiet. Unfortunately, the three of you started mucking around in here, and—"

"Hey! We're not a bunch of meddlesome kids joyriding in your stupid Book," interrupted Sabrina. "We're trying to rescue our brother. Once we find him, we'll go."

The Editor closed his eyes and sighed deeply. "This brother of yours . . . I can feel his presence in the Book, along with two others—the Magic Mirror and Pinocchio."

"Mirror kidnapped our brother, and Pinocchio helped him. We're not leaving without him," Daphne said.

The Editor frowned, leaning back in his chair. "I can have you removed," he said matter-of-factly.

"Go ahead. We'll just come back," Daphne said. "And next time we can make things even harder for you."

"We'll wreck every story in this book," Puck threatened.

"I cannot allow it," the Editor snapped. "Leave now, or my revisers will devour you."

Puck shrugged. "I've been eaten before. It's no big deal."

Daphne pulled Puck and Sabrina back toward the red door. She opened it, and a terrible wind tugged at their clothes and hair.

"You are making a terrible mistake!" the Editor warned.

"If I had a nickel for every time a bad guy told me that, I'd be one rich detective," Daphne said. She pulled everyone through the doorway. With a whoosh, the library was gone.

Sabrina found herself standing on a large flat rock beneath an inky night sky. The air was hot and humid, and she could smell wild creatures nearby. She held a torch. Its red flame illuminated the pack of wolves that encircled her. Their eyes were locked on the ground, and many were trembling.

"Thou art the master," a voice called from the trees above her. When she looked up, Sabrina spotted a black panther nestled in the branches. "Save Akela from the death. He was ever your friend."

Terrified, Sabrina screamed and stumbled backward, expecting the panther to pounce. When it didn't, she tried to calm down by whispering to herself over and over again that she was in a story and that story animals were not the same as their man-eating real-life versions. At least, she hoped not. The fact that the panther was talking to her was a good sign, too. Most of the talking animals in Ferryport Landing weren't savage—annoying, but not bloodthirsty.

Unfortunately, nothing was certain. Daphne and Puck were nowhere in sight. Perhaps they had been the panther's appetizers, and she was the main course.

"Daphne? Puck? I could really use some help here," Sabrina called tentatively.

An old gray wolf stood nearby. Its head was bowed low in submission like the others', but it looked up in confusion when Sabrina spoke. "What did the man-cub say?"

"I have no idea," another wolf said.

"Could the man-cub repeat himself?" a third asked.

"Man-cub?" Sabrina was becoming even more confused.

Just then, a figure crawled toward her on its hands and knees. Sabrina scrambled backward until she heard it giggle.

"Daphne!" Sabrina cried. "You scared me to death!"

Daphne stood and revealed her smiling face. "We're in *The Jungle Book*! I'm a wolf!" She took a deep breath and let out a goofy howl. It sounded less like a wolf and more like an injured house cat. But the rest of the pack followed suit and wailed at the full moon.

"I think the Book turned you into Mowgli! Nice outfit," the little girl giggled.

Sabrina looked at herself and realized she was wearing a kind of dress made from animal skins.

"Oh, brother," she groaned, then searched her memory for facts about Mowgli. She had skipped the book, but Granny spoke of it frequently. She remembered that Mowgli was a boy from India raised by wolves. His friends were a bear and a panther, and there was something about a tiger—but Sabrina couldn't remember anything specific. Was the tiger really annoying and hyperactive and bouncing around a lot? Maybe that was from another story.

"Where's Puck?" Sabrina asked.

Daphne shrugged. "He's around here somewhere."

Sabrina frowned as she studied the wolf pack. "Any idea what we should do before we're turned into dog food?"

"Excuse me?" one of the wolves cried. "We're not dogs, we're wolves!"

"And, please, try to say your lines," another wolf complained. "If you skip them, I will get lost and forget mine."

The wolves fell silent when a huge, muscled animal lumbered onto the rock. Sabrina nearly dropped her torch when she realized it was a Bengal tiger. It hobbled on a lame foot, but it was still utterly terrifying.

"Enough!" the tiger roared. "You are messing up this story. Mowgli, you will grant Akela a pardon from death and then accept your banishment from the pack and the Council. Then, you must attack some of the wolves with your torch and then attack me. You must stick to the story, or I will kill you where you stand, man-cub."

"First of all, I'm not a 'man-cub.' If anything, I'm a woman-cub," Sabrina snapped. "Second of all, I don't know this story well enough to follow it, so you're going to have to cut me a break."

The wolves began whispering among themselves.

"He's arguing with Shere Khan."

"Is he trying to get himself killed?"

"Perhaps pain will help you remember your role, Mowgli," Shere Khan threatened, flashing the claws on one of his good paws.

Something dropped out of the sky and landed between the girls and the tiger. It pointed a wooden sword at Shere Khan.

"Keep your paws off my fiancée," Puck shouted.

"By the Broken Lock that freed me!" the panther cried as he eyed the boy fairy. "Who are you?"

Puck puffed up his chest. "I am the Trickster King. Leader of the Lazy, Master of Mayhem—surely you've heard of me."

The wolves exchanged confused glances and shook their heads. "Are you one of the Monkey People?"

"No! I am the sworn protector of the Grimms, and you will not touch them."

Shere Khan roared so powerfully that Puck's hair blew into an even bigger mess than usual.

"Whoever you are, you are ruining the story!" Shere Khan bellowed. "The Editor will not tolerate it, and I have no intention of being revised."

The tiger leaped forward with his razor-sharp claws extended. He slashed at the fairy, but Puck dodged the mighty blow. Puck struck back, but his tiny weapon was deflected by a vicious swat. It flew out of his hand and disappeared into the tall grass. Shere Khan pounced again, slashing Puck's hoodie to ribbons.

"Puck!" Sabrina cried.

Puck was rattled, but he quickly recovered his composure. He unfurled his wings and flapped until he hovered above the angry tiger.

"He may not be real, but his claws sure are," Puck told the girls. "All right, kitty cat, now you've really got the attention of the true King of Fairies."

"Come down here, mosquito, so I can finish what I've started," Shere Khan raged.

"Fine with me. I need a new rug for my bedroom anyway," Puck said, and then he swooped down, snatched up his sword from the grass, and rocketed straight toward the massive beast. He swung his weapon hard into Shere Khan's spine, and the cat cried in agony before falling to the ground.

"If I were you, I'd slink back home for a bowl of milk," Puck mocked.

Shere Khan lumbered to his feet. His fur glowed in the moonlight, and his eyes smoldered like hot coals. In one sudden movement, he leaped at a tree, bouncing off of it and launching himself at Puck. Shere Khan slashed at the fairy's chest as Puck kicked desperately at the tiger's face. Shere Khan's claws missed Puck's skin by a fraction of an inch.

Sabrina was shocked. She'd assumed the trio couldn't be hurt inside the stories. All of it had seemed like pretend. The risk of injury or death added yet another fear to her rapidly growing list.

It was Puck's turn to fight back. He flew at Shere Khan, but the tiger caught him with a well-timed punch. The boy fairy fell from the sky and rolled into Sabrina, knocking the torch from her grasp. It dropped onto the flat, smooth rock and rolled into a patch of tall grass nearby. A moment later, the grass burst into hungry flames.

"What have you done?" the black panther cried.

"What have *I* done?" Sabrina repeated. "The tiger is the one causing the problems!"

The old wolf stepped forward to address the other wolves. "Flee, brothers. The Red Flower is blossoming."

The wolves howled and darted away from the spreading fire. The panther leaped down from his tree and followed them.

"What red flower?" Sabrina asked.

"They're talking about the fire," Daphne said. "It's what the animals call a flame in the book, but this didn't happen in the story. It wouldn't have been very good if Mowgli torched the forest and killed everything within miles."

"Speak for yourself," Puck said, still wrestling with Shere Khan. "That story would rule."

"What should we do?" Sabrina asked.

"I vote for running!" Daphne shouted.

"Duh!" Puck exclaimed, freeing himself from the tiger's grasp.

The trio stomped through the brush, racing after the fleeing animals. Shere Khan leaped into their path and stared them down with his murderous eyes.

"You have doomed us all," he growled. "The Editor and his revisers will be here any moment, but perhaps he will spare me if I kill those responsible for the damage."

Shere Khan leaped at them, swatting with his massive paws, but Puck snatched each of the girls by the back of their shirts and flew them skyward just in time. "If Garfield won't let us pass, I suppose we'll just have to take another route."

"Thanks," Sabrina said. "That was a close one."

"No problem, darling," Puck crowed. "I can't exactly let my bride-to-be become a cat toy."

A stone sailed through the air and slammed into Puck's head, nearly knocking the trio out of the sky. In the treetops below, hundreds of monkeys were swinging from limbs and vines, shaking angry fists at them.

"Those must be the Monkey People," Daphne said.

More rocks sailed in their direction. Puck did his best to avoid them, but there were too many to dodge. He was forced to fly higher.

"How does this story end?" Sabrina asked. "We should find the magic door and get out of here."

"That depends," Daphne said. "*The Jungle Book* isn't just one story. It's a collection of short stories. Technically, this part is over. The door might be down there now."

"Puck, we have to go back down," Sabrina commanded.

"You want me to fly us down into that inferno filled with evil monkeys?" Puck said. "You're completely insane!"

"A good quality in a wife," Daphne said.

"Good point, marshmallow," Puck said. "Hold on, folks. We're in for a bumpy landing!"

Puck stopped flapping his wings, and the trio plummeted toward the ground. Sabrina braced herself for a nasty collision with the jungle floor, but the boy fairy suddenly expanded his wings to slow their descent.

"Do you see a door?" Daphne asked as their feet touched ground.

"It could be anywhere," Sabrina said frantically. She felt as though things couldn't get any worse for them. But the Book of Everafter felt differently. Suddenly, a herd of long-horned cattle stampeded out of the trees. They tore through the jungle, destroying everything in their wake. Their panicked cries rose above the roar of the crackling fire. The children leaped behind an ancient tree for protection, only to spot another wave of cattle approaching from the opposite direction. Nowhere was safe.

Puck spun around on his heels and transformed into a gorilla with thick black fur and huge, muscled arms. He tossed Daphne onto one shoulder and Sabrina onto the other, climbed a tree, and perched them all on a high branch. A moment later, he morphed back to his true form.

"We'll be safe here," Puck assured them.

"Are you sure?" Daphne asked. "Look!"

Within the stampede, Sabrina spotted a group of creatures altogether unlike the cows. They were small, pink, and fast.

"Revisers!" she cried.

The little monsters devoured everything they touched. The children watched the jungle around them disappear. It was replaced with an empty white void, like a blank sheet of paper.

"I'm so going to have nightmares like this!" Daphne shouted.

"OK, new plan. Let's get back in the air," Sabrina said.

Puck unfurled his wings, and soon the trio was rocketing out of the tree line, high above the hungry revisers. But Sabrina still didn't feel safe. The entire world was vanishing before her eyes: The trees, the animals, and even the night sky were being gobbled up and replaced with nothingness. The Editor's words echoed in her mind.

Leave now, or my revisers will devour you.

Daphne's eyes were wide with fear. "They're very fast."

"Don't worry. I'm faster!" Puck shouted. "Besides, I couldn't let anything happen to my fiancée and my future sister-in-law! While we're on the subject, I was hoping we could discuss our wedding cake. I think we should go traditional—you know, something stuffed with rubber doggie poo. What do you think, honey? Of course, I have always wanted a cake made out of hot dogs. Then it would match your dress!"

"You keep flapping your mouth, fairy, and I'm going to marry my fist to your face," Sabrina threatened.

"There's the door!" Daphne shouted, pointing to a ridge below them. Something red stood among the bushes—something that clearly didn't belong there. Daphne was right: It was a door, but the revisers were practically on top of it. If they destroyed it, would there be any way to get out of the story?

"Puck! Go! Now!" Sabrina cried.

Puck sped them toward the door like a bullet. Still, the revisers were everywhere, piling up in front of the portal, blocking their exit.

"You're not going to do what I think you are," Daphne yelled over the wind.

Puck laughed. "I think you already know the answer to that!"

He flew right through the revisers like a cannonball, scattering the monsters left and right. The children skidded to a stop at the door and scrambled to their feet. Without stopping to think, Sabrina opened the door and pushed the others through the portal.

She was about to jump in after them when one of the revisers leaped at her. She caught it in her hands, and it snapped and growled, struggling to sink its teeth into her flesh. She threw it away from her, back into the pack of monsters, and scurried toward the door. It was then that she saw something she didn't quite understand. Something was killing the revisers. It was completely invisible yet vicious and destructive. It slashed and killed some revisers, and many of the grotesque creatures flew rapidly from the unseen assailant.

As curious as she was, Sabrina knew better than to stick around. She crawled on hands and knees through the doorway, and *The Jungle Book* vanished.

3

SABRINA STOOD AT THE EDGE OF ANOTHER dark, unfamiliar forest. But unlike that of *The Jungle Book*, this one smelled of cedar pines. The air was crisp and cool, and a layer of early-morning dew coated the ground. The change of scenery was welcome. There seemed to be no angry tigers, hungry monsters, or invisible warriors around.

Daphne stood nearby, dressed in a new outfit—a puffy shirt and royal-blue leggings. When Sabrina looked down, she realized she was wearing a similar outfit, and she sighed in relief. She was glad to be rid of the animal skins.

Puck was still in his hoodie.

"How come you never change?" Sabrina asked him.

He shrugged. "You can't improve on perfection."

"I have a theory," Daphne said. "His story is in this book. Maybe he doesn't change because he's supposed to be in here. We're not, so the book has to make room for us."

"Which story is this one anyway?" Puck asked.

Daphne discovered a sword sheathed at her side. She took it out and awkwardly swung it around. "Maybe we're in *The Three Musketeers*! I hope I'm D'Artagnan. Hey, that's a good name for the baby. D'Artagnan Grimm!"

"First, ugh. Second, I don't think this is *The Three Musketeers*," Sabrina said, pointing to a crowd of men in similar outfits. Each had shoulder-length hair and a full beard. Leading the group along a well-worn path was a woman wearing rich, embroidered robes. A golden crown adorned with delicate jewels rested on her head. Her face, however, was not so delicate. It was sharp and angry, and it was pointed right at the trio.

"No one speaks during this part," the queen whispered.

"Sorry," Daphne whispered back, and then turned back to Sabrina and Puck. "Looks like we have to stick to the script again."

They followed the crowd through the forest until they reached an overgrown part of the path. The queen held up her hand, and her men came to an abrupt stop. While everyone watched, the queen reached into the folds of her robes and took out a ball of white yarn. She raised it to her mouth and whispered something into it. Then she set it on the ground and stood back. The yarn twitched and hopped, bouncing around like a Mexican jumping bean. Suddenly, it chose a direction and rolled farther into the woods, leaving a strand in its wake. The queen picked up the loose end of yarn and followed it into the forest. As she walked, she collected the loose strand and wrapped it into a new ball.

"Ahhh, now I know where we are," Daphne said. "This is 'The Six Swans.'"

Sabrina hadn't read 'The Six Swans.' She hadn't even skimmed through it.

"That woman is a witch," Daphne explained. "Her husband is a king, and he has seven children by his first wife. The witch wants to do bad things to her stepkids, so the king hid them in a cabin in the woods. The ball of magic yarn will help her find their hiding place."

"So the yarn is like a GPS device or something?" Sabrina asked.

One of the queen's men shot them an angry look. "Shhhhh!"

"Yes," Daphne whispered to her sister.

Soon, they came across a cottage built on the banks of a bubbling spring. Six smiling boys, the oldest the same age as Sabrina, raced out of the cabin toward the group. They were eager to greet their visitors, but when they saw the queen, their joyful faces fell in fear. They tried to flee, but the queen's men pounced on them before they could get very far. The men dragged the boys back to their wicked stepmother.

Once more, the witch reached into the folds of her dress, this time removing six silk shirts. One by one she dressed the boys in them, and, with a flash of light, each went through a transformation. Legs and arms vanished. Lean bodies plumped up and sprouted feathers. Shoes were replaced with webbed feet. They were no longer boys but frightened white swans.

"She turned them into birds!" Sabrina cried, shuddering at the memory of her own recent metamorphosis into a goose. "What happens next?"

"I don't remember exactly, but I think their sister finds a way to break the spell," Daphne said. "But she has to keep quiet for six years to do it."

"What did you say?" a voice snapped.

The girls turned to find the queen standing behind them, listening to every word they said.

"Did you say the king has another child?" she continued.

"Um," Daphne said.

"I'm not supposed to know that!"

"You could pretend you didn't hear it," Sabrina suggested.

The queen shook her head. "No, I can't. Now it's part of the story. And I can't just let her go—it won't make any sense. I have to go in there and turn her into a swan, too. The whole tale will be different now. You're going to bring the Editor down on us!"

The guards yelped and fled into the woods as if running for their lives. The queen raced after them, dropping her ball of yarn in her haste.

"We're sorry!" Daphne shouted after them.

"Messing up these stories is kind of fun." Puck chuckled.

Sabrina snatched the abandoned yarn and immediately felt the uncomfortable sensation she always experienced when handling magical items. She quickly handed it to Daphne.

"Wow! There's some serious mojo coming off of this thing, even more than Dorothy's slippers," Daphne said. She examined the yarn closely, then held it to her mouth. "Take us to Mirror."

Like before, the ball fell to the ground, bounced and popped, then rolled into the woods. Sabrina watched in amazement.

"Daphne! You're brilliant!"

"I know." Daphne shrugged.

The children chased the rolling ball of yarn through the woods, rewrapping the loose end as they went. The faster they ran, the faster the yarn seemed to roll, until it zipped down a dry creek bed where a red door materialized. The yarn stopped in front of the door and hopped around as if eager to keep moving.

"Wait! I thought we needed to go to the end of a story to find a magic door," Daphne said.

"Just open it," Sabrina said. "Something is finally going our way."

Daphne opened the door, and the wind that hit them smelled like leather and burning wood. Sabrina recognized it immediately.

"No, I was wrong! Close the door!" Sabrina cried.

Daphne tried to shove the door closed, but the wind was too powerful. The yarn rolled through the doorway and disappeared. Then, an unseen force dragged the children through, as well.

When she opened her eyes, Sabrina found herself lying flat on her back in the Editor's library. The man himself was sitting in his leather chair nearby. He was flipping through the dry pages of an old book. He paused to look down at her and cocked a curious eyebrow. Sabrina scrambled to her feet and prepared to fight.

"Calm down, young lady," the Editor demanded.

"Don't you 'young lady' me," Sabrina snapped.

Daphne and Puck got to their feet, fists clenched.

"I have no desire to attack you." The Editor sighed. "I want to hire you."

The trio shared incredulous glances as the man stood and poked at some dying embers in his fireplace. Sparks flew in every direction as the flames grew. As he stoked the fire, Sabrina noticed a dozen or so revisers scurrying around the room. They clambered up the shelves like overfed spiders and melted into the shadows.

"You want to hire us?" Sabrina asked.

"You are detectives, correct? The last Grimm who traipsed through these pages claimed it was a family business."

"Who are you talking about?" Daphne asked.

"She called herself Trixie Grimm," he replied.

"Great-Aunt Trixie," Daphne said.

"I find myself in a most peculiar situation that requires your particular set of skills," he said. "I want you to find a trespasser within the Book, the Everafter known as Pinocchio."

"I almost forgot he came in here with us," Puck said. "Is he mucking up the book, too?"

The Editor nodded. "While you three are ruining some stories, he's causing mayhem in others. Since you are so-called detectives, I'd like to hire you to chase him down and help me remove him."

"Wait! Doesn't he have a right to be in here?" Daphne asked warily. "He's allowed to change his story if he wants to."

The Editor sat back down in his chair. He petted a reviser that scurried out from under a nearby sofa. It panted with its long tongue hanging out, happy for its master's attention. "Yes, well, after much thought I have decided that this particular practice must come to an end. The last time someone changed their story, there were disastrous consequences for both this world and your own. I cannot allow it to happen again."

"We're not interested," Sabrina said. "While we're busy hunting down Pinocchio, Mirror will get to his own story. He's planning to make changes that will hurt our family, and we can't give up our only chance to stop him. The puppet is your problem."

"Don't be so hasty, sugar bear," Puck said with a devilish grin. "He said he wants to hire us. We could use the money for our wedding. Ice sculptures of minotaurs are not cheap, and of course there's the fire pit for guests who bring lousy gifts. We really could use the cash."

Sabrina scowled.

"Mirror will never reach his story," the Editor said.

"I wouldn't bet on that, mister," Daphne said.

"His story is off-limits. It was locked tight by powerful magic. No one can enter it, not even my revisers. So you three can stop worrying about Mirror and help me find Pinocchio. Once he's been removed from this book, I will take you to Mirror. And I will help you rescue the infant from him. Do we have a deal?"

Sabrina looked at her sister. "What do you think?"

"If what he says is true and Mirror can't change his story, I think we should help. Plus, it would be nice to not worry about those things anymore," Daphne said, pointing to the reviser at the Editor's feet.

"Unfortunately, I cannot call off the revisers. They are like white blood cells protecting the human body. When something from outside comes into these pages, the revisers treat it like a virus, attacking until it is completely gone. I cannot change their function."

"So even though we're trying to help, they might still eat us?" Puck asked.

The Editor nodded.

"I'm in," Puck said. "It's kind of exciting to be back on the food chain. Plus, if I get a chance to punch Pinocchio in his stupid, pointy nose, then it's worth it."

Daphne nodded. "He shouldn't be too hard to find. We know he's headed for his own story."

"Do you swear you'll help us stop Mirror?" Sabrina asked.

"You have my word," the Editor said, and then he waved his hand, and a red door appeared. The door opened, and the gust of wind that blasted Sabrina's hair back smelled sweaty and pungent, like bad body odor. "Now, if the terms of our agreement are satisfactory, I suggest you get started right away. Use the ball of yarn you found in 'The Six Swans' to your advantage. It will lead you from door to door more quickly than following the stories. When you find our enemy, call out to me. I can hear everything you say. I will send you a door that leads back here to my library. Oh, and don't forget Pinocchio's marionettes, either. They are as damaging to these stories as their master."

"We'll do our best," Daphne said.

"You have my every confidence," said the Editor. "This door will take you to Pinocchio."

"Hey, one last thing," Sabrina said as they stepped toward the portal. "One of the Munchkins told us to stay inside the margins of the story. What does that mean?"

"That's correct. Do not traipse through parts of any story that the original author did not write. Those are wild places, and something evil lives there . . . something you do not want to meet. Even I do not risk stepping into its domain. You encountered it, didn't you, Sabrina Grimm?"

Sabrina nodded. Something had slaughtered the revisers in *The Jungle Book*. At first, she'd thought perhaps it was trying to help her, but now she wasn't so sure.

Sabrina stepped into a milky fog. It danced and swirled around her. She could barely see her hands in front of her, but the whole experience was calming and oddly beautiful. The ground beneath her was strange, as well. It felt spongy, like she was standing on a giant slice of angel food cake.

"Uh, are we in heaven?" Daphne asked from somewhere nearby.

"No chance of that. I doubt they'd let me in," Puck chimed in. "The ground is kind of strange. It's like we're walking around on someone's belly."

"It's more like I'm walking on the moon," Daphne said, jumping up and down. "This is one small step for man, one giant leap for Daphne!"

"Cool it!" Sabrina snapped. "We have no idea what story we're in right now. The less attention we draw to ourselves, the better."

Daphne jumped one last time and landed with an "Ouch!"

"What's wrong?" cried Sabrina.

"I just landed on something hard," Daphne said. She reached down and pulled up a burlap sack. It looked heavy. She dipped her hands into the bag and pulled out a fistful of gold coins.

"We're rich!" Puck cried. "We can use it for our wedding, sweetums."

Sabrina flushed. Puck's wedding-day jokes had been infuriating at first, but now they were getting embarrassing. She could throw another insult his way, but she just felt confused and shy.

"Why is there a bag of gold just lying here?" Daphne asked. "And what's with all this fog? Does this remind you of any fairy tales?"

Just then, there was an enormous crash, and the ground beneath them shifted. All three children toppled over.

"What was that?" Puck cried.

An angry bellow rang out. It sounded almost human, but it was louder than anything Sabrina had ever heard. It raised the hair on her arms and sent shivers racing along her spine.

"I don't think we should stick around to find out," Sabrina said, frantically helping Daphne and Puck to their feet.

"No, it's cool. Just relax," Puck said, a grin spreading across his face.

"Relax? You heard that roar, right?" Daphne asked.

"That wasn't a roar. Were you listening to him?" Puck asked.

"Him?" Sabrina said.

"Yep, him. The big guy is angry. He just said, 'Fe, fi, fo, fum.'"

Sabrina started to panic. The last thing they needed right now was a run-in with giants! She'd killed one on her second day in Ferryport Landing and never wanted to meet another.

"That explains the fog," Puck said. "We're standing on a cloud. We're in the giants' kingdom."

"Run!" Sabrina shouted.

Puck called to her to stop, but Sabrina had grabbed Daphne's hand, and they were already sprinting ahead. A shoe the size of a battleship came crashing down in front of them, blocking their path. They turned and ran in the opposite direction, right past Puck.

"Where do the two of you think you're going to run? You're in the sky!" he shouted.

Sabrina didn't care. She just wanted to get away. She looked around for a hiding place or a way out and spotted the top of an enormous beanstalk breaking through the clouds. She remembered Jack's story—Jack, who traded his family's cow for magic beans. Overnight, they grew into a giant beanstalk. It led to a kingdom in the clouds.

If it went up, she thought, *it must go down*.

Sabrina headed for Jack's beanstalk, pulling Daphne along with her. As they got closer, she noticed someone else had chosen the same escape route. A lone figure was shimmying down the bean-stalk. He wore bright blue overalls and couldn't have been more than three feet tall.

"Who's that climbing down the beanstalk?" Daphne asked, pointing ahead of them.

"Pinocchio!" Sabrina cried.

The boy must have heard her, as he redoubled his efforts to es-cape. Seeing him again, after his betrayal of her family and friends, motivated Sabrina even further. Maybe it was anger, maybe it was a desire for revenge, but suddenly her fear of the giant vanished. All she wanted now was to make the little punk pay.

When the children reached the beanstalk, Sabrina grabbed on to a thick leaf and was surprised to find it was sticky. She low-ered herself to the next leaf, then the next. Daphne followed, then Puck. Soon, the three were steadily descending from the giants' kingdom in the clouds and into the open air. Far below, they saw a tiny cottage on an overgrown farm.

Daphne gulped loudly in fear.

"Don't look down!" Sabrina said to her.

"Actually, looking down is a very good idea! Watch out!" Daphne wailed, pointing past Sabrina.

Crawling up toward the trio at an amazing speed were six wooden marionettes, which Pinocchio had carved to look like members of the Grimm family: Henry, Veronica, Granny Relda,

Uncle Jake, Daphne, and Sabrina. They leaped from leaf to leaf like monkeys, reaching the children in no time. Without hesitation, they attacked viciously, punching and kicking with their sharp little hands and feet. Their assault was more painful than Sabrina expected. One well-placed hit to her eye left her momentarily blinded, but she managed to hang on to the beanstalk.

With her free hand, Sabrina swiped at the marionette that looked like her and flung it from the vine. It fell silently past its comrades, who watched in horror. The one that looked like Uncle Jake stomped down hard on Daphne's fingers, and she lost her grip. She fell into the open sky and plummeted toward the ground.

4

BEFORE SABRINA COULD EVEN SCREAM, PUCK leaped off the beanstalk and dove down toward Daphne. Sabrina watched him, her heart pounding. She saw his pink wings expand and flutter in the wind, but she couldn't see if he had caught her sister. She closed her eyes tightly and begged the heavens for Daphne's life.

"Here's the piglet," Puck said. Sabrina opened her eyes to find him hovering in front of her, holding Daphne. She reached out to Sabrina, who caught her and held on like she might never let Daphne go.

"You have to be more careful," Sabrina scolded her sister.

"I will," Daphne whimpered.

An enormous boot dug into the beanstalk just above them. Stuck in its heel was what looked like the bodies of forest animals and even a few human skeletons. A horrible, rotting funk wafted across Sabrina's face,

"I smell the blood of an Englishman!" the giant bellowed.

"It's not us! We're from the Upper East Side of Manhattan!" Sabrina shouted, scrambling down the vine as fast as she could without losing her grip on the beanstalk or her sister.

But she wasn't fast enough. The giant scooped Sabrina and Daphne into one tight, sweaty fist and lifted them up until they were level with his gruesome face. A tangle of overgrown hairs sprouted from his nose, and each of his broken teeth was a different shade of brown. The stench of his breath rivaled the smell from his boot.

"Don't worry. I've got this," Puck said as he flew casually over to the giant's ear. He shouted something into it that the girls could not hear. The giant grunted back at Puck, and then the fairy fluttered back down to them. "Allow me to introduce you to my new assistant."

"What are you talking about?" Sabrina cried.

"I just recruited some help. Try to keep up, ugly," Puck said.

"Friends!" the giant roared. Then, with a sudden jerk, he began descending the rest of the beanstalk. In no time at all, the giant had climbed all the way down, though he still held Sabrina and Daphne at least ten feet off the ground.

The girls peered up at him suspiciously, unsure whether to trust Puck and stay put or jump down and run for their lives. Neither option seemed like a safe bet.

Puck pointed across the farm. Pinocchio and his marionettes were bolting into the forest. "Hey, big guy, you see that boy running across the field?"

The giant grunted.

"That's Jack. He's the guy who stole your stuff."

The giant growled furiously and took off after Pinocchio, stomping on the little house in his dash across the farm. Every step caused the girls to bounce around violently.

"Good thinking," Daphne said to the fairy. "You know, sometimes you're . . . you're Pucktastic!"

"That's not a word," Sabrina said, rolling her eyes. Sometimes Daphne's vocabulary seemed to materialize out of thin air.

"It is now! It means something is awesome in the best possible way."

"Works for me!" Puck crowed.

Suddenly, the giant stopped. He spun around and set the sisters on the ground. When Sabrina got her bearings, she saw Pinocchio running toward them. They were blocking his escape.

"Step aside, brute," Pinocchio demanded.

"Fe! Fi! Fo! Fum!" the giant bellowed. "I smell the blood of an Englishman."

"You big idiot," the boy mocked. "I'm not part of your story."

Puck fluttered to the giant's ear. "Don't listen to him. He's Jack! Jack the Giant Killer! You know, as in a killer of giants."

The giant roared and beat his chest like an oversized gorilla. Pinocchio stomped the ground in fury and stretched out his arm. He was holding a long black wand with a crystal star on its end. It crackled and popped with magical energy. Pinocchio flicked it hard, and a lightning bolt shot at the giant, hitting him squarely in the chest. The giant bellowed as he staggered back a step, though Sabrina couldn't tell if it was from pain or anger. He looked genuinely perplexed that such a small creature could hurt him.

"Where did he get that?" Daphne asked.

"He must have swiped it from one of the stories," Sabrina said.

"Of course I did," Pinocchio snapped. "I would have to be a fool not to take full advantage of being in these stories. I liberated this from Cinderella's fairy godmother."

"It's going to take more than a sparkler to stop our friend here," Puck said, and then turned to the giant. "Hey, big guy! That's the fellow who stole the goose that lays the golden eggs!"

The giant roared again and leaped forward, only to be met with another painful shock. He doubled over and fell to one knee.

"Puppet boy has to go down," Daphne said.

She scooped up a rock. Puck took out his wooden sword. Sabrina clenched her hands into fists.

"Let's do it," Sabrina said with a grin. While Pinocchio was distracted, the trio attacked. Puck smacked Pinocchio in the mouth with his sword. Daphne kicked him in the shins. Sabrina punched and slapped anything she could reach. The little boy was forced to halt his attack on the giant. When he saw he was outnumbered, he rushed into the woods. The children chased him up ridges and across creek beds until they finally found him in a clearing. A magic door was waiting. He opened it and turned to face them.

"It would be ill-advised for you miscreants to continue pursuing me," the boy said.

"What did he say?" Puck asked.

"Who knows?" Daphne replied.

"Philistines!" Pinocchio cried, and then he stepped through the doorway and vanished.

"What does *philistines* mean?" Daphne asked.

Sabrina shrugged. "My best guess is he's calling us morons. Come on, let's follow him."

Sabrina reached for the doorknob, but when she grasped it, it vanished in her hand. So did the door.

"Uh-oh," Puck said.

"What do we do now?" Daphne asked.

Before Sabrina could answer, the giant lowered his head so that he could speak to the group.

"Oohg want to say thanks," the giant said. "You make Oohg happy."

"Happy? How?" Daphne asked.

"Oohg stomp through story many times. Each time, Jack kill Oohg. This time, Oohg survive."

Sabrina frowned. "I'm afraid the Editor will come and fix that."

"Editor can try. Until then, Oohg enjoy new ending. Also, Oohg very honored to take part in celebration."

"Huh?"

"Meet my best man," Puck said, gesturing grandly at the giant. "See you at the church, pal!"

The giant nodded respectfully and stomped back the way he'd come, pulverizing trees with his enormous boots.

"Daphne like Oohg," the little girl said, mimicking the giant's way of speaking. "Hey! How does Oohg Grimm sound for the baby's name?"

Sabrina rolled her eyes. "C'mon, we need to focus on getting out of this story. Revisers will be here soon. We wrecked this story, and our new boss is not going to be happy about it."

"Let's use the yarn," Daphne said, reaching into her pocket for the magical tool.

"We need a new door," she said to it, and then set it on the ground. It took off, speeding toward the woods.

The children followed the yarn's trail for a long time, but soon they grew tired and hungry. In a shady, cool part of the woods they found a pear tree. Puck shook its trunk, and plump, juicy fruit fell from the branches. The children washed the fruit in a nearby pond and then sat down to feast.

"I don't remember this forest in Jack's story," Daphne said.

Sabrina nodded in agreement. "I think we're in the margins," she explained.

"But the Editor told us to stay out of the margins," Daphne said, her brow furrowing.

"Well, the yarn is saying something else," Sabrina said as her sister finished winding it up. "You two get some rest. I'll take the first watch."

Puck and Daphne didn't argue. Soon, both were snoring loudly. To keep herself awake, Sabrina practiced skipping stones on the pond.

After a few failed attempts, she managed to get one to skip three times before it sank. She searched for more stones, collecting them in the belly of her shirt. When she turned back to the pond, she dropped them all to the ground in shock. Before her loomed a creature made of water. It was shaped like a man, and it had leaves and pebbles swirling around inside its body. It raced toward Sabrina, and—before she could react—it was on top of her, its cold, wet hands around her throat.

"Free me!" it bellowed in an inhuman voice. "Release me from this prison!"

Suddenly, a blast of flame engulfed the creature. It lost its shape and cried out, releasing Sabrina. She scrambled to her feet and found Puck standing behind her, breathing fire at the monster. It boiled into steam and, soon, disappeared completely.

"What was that thing, Grimm?" Puck asked.

"I think that thing is why everyone has been warning us about the margins," Sabrina croaked. "It demanded that I set it free."

"What's going on?" Daphne asked as she rushed to the pond.

"Nothing," Sabrina said quickly. She flashed Puck a look, hoping he'd understand that she didn't want to scare her little sister. He shrugged and kept quiet.

"Well, come on. The ball of yarn is practically leaping out of my pocket," Daphne said, then tossed it to the ground. Like before, it raced off at top speed.

The trio followed. The ball took them out of the woods, then through a lawn thick with tall grass, and finally to a familiar farm with a crushed house. Next to it, the enormous beanstalk rose up into the clouds.

"It brought us back to Jack's place," Puck said. "Why?"

"'Cause the story isn't complete," Daphne explained. "Remember what the Munchkins told us: We have to finish the story to get a door to the next one."

"How do we end this disaster?" Sabrina wondered aloud. "We have no Jack and no giant."

"But there's one thing we can finish," Daphne said, pointing at the beanstalk. "We have to chop that down."

Sabrina looked around, then walked over and grabbed an ax she found resting against a tree. She tried to hand it to Puck, but he wouldn't take it.

"This smells suspiciously like work, and you know I'm allergic."

"We have to try," Sabrina argued. "Besides, I'd like to get out of here as soon as possible."

Puck grumbled and snatched the ax from her hands. He marched up to the enormous plant and swung wildly. Eventually, the beanstalk fell over, crushing what little was left of Jack's house.

Thankfully, Daphne was right—felling the beanstalk marked the end of the story. A new red door materialized immediately.

Without hesitation, Sabrina pulled it open. This time, the wind smelled like wild grass and tea. Daphne whispered for the ball of yarn to follow Pinocchio, and it rolled into the void. The trio took one another by the hand and once again stepped into the unknown.

Sabrina sat at a long wooden table set beneath a tall tree. A little cottage stood nearby, and wildflowers sprouted in every direction.

When Sabrina noticed who was sitting with her, she nearly fell from her chair. The Mad Hatter faced her, sipping tea from a massive cup and resting his elbow on poor Daphne's head. On Daphne's other side sat a brown rabbit at least as tall as she. He rested his elbow on Daphne's head, too. The little girl looked annoyed as she squirmed and struggled to escape. Puck, however, was enjoying himself. He sat next to Sabrina and was already shoveling handfuls of cake into his mouth. All the while, the magic ball of yarn zipped into the woods, leaving its trail behind.

Sabrina looked down at herself. She was wearing a blue dress and a frilly apron. She knew—without a doubt—exactly which story they were in.

"We're in Wonderland," Sabrina whispered, panic rising in her throat.

"Shhhhhhhh!" the Mad Hatter snapped. "Stick to the story, young lady."

"Have some wine," the rabbit said.

"Wine? Where do you think we are, France? I'm twelve years old," Sabrina argued.

The rabbit let out a little yelp of fear. Clearly, the March Hare and the Mad Hatter were afraid of the Editor, too.

"You're supposed to be Alice," Daphne reminded her.

"Fine, fine, but Alice was even younger in her story. Who are these two hooligans offering me alcohol?"

The Hatter and the Hare looked upset, but they said nothing to defend themselves.

"Do you know this story?" Daphne whispered to Sabrina.

"I read it a few times during Mr. Canis's trial. I wanted to understand the way the Hatter thinks," she explained.

"And what did you find out?" Daphne asked.

"That he doesn't," she said. "But the whole story's super weird.

I had to go over it again and again. Everyone is insane, and they talk a lot of nonsense."

"So they're just like you," Puck teased between greedy bites.

"Your hair wants cutting," the Hatter said abruptly.

Sabrina rolled her eyes at Daphne. "See?"

"Say something to him," Daphne whispered.

"I don't remember what I'm supposed to say," Sabrina complained.

The Mad Hatter and the March Hare shared a worried look until the Hare whispered, "You're supposed to say, 'You should learn not to make personal remarks. It's very rude.'"

Sabrina sighed and repeated the lines to the Mad Hatter.

"Why is a raven like a writing-desk?" he asked.

"I can't do this," Sabrina said, slamming her hands on the table as she stood. "He's talking in riddles, and I hate riddles. Let's skip this part."

"Skip it?" the Mad Hatter said as he stood, alarmed. He dropped his teacup, and it shattered on the table.

"You fool!" the Hare cried. "That didn't happen in the story. The Editor will be after us now."

"She made me do it!" the Hatter cried as he pointed a shaky finger at Sabrina.

"That doesn't matter; you still changed the story!" the March Hare cried. "What were you thinking? Well, I won't suffer for your mistakes. When the beasties arrive, I will tell them what you have done."

"Throw me under the bus, will you!" the Mad Hatter shouted.

"Why should I be revised? I'm innocent!" the Hare said.

The Hatter grabbed the Hare by the neck and shook him, hard. Enraged, the Hare swung wildly and hit the old man in the eye. The force sent the Hatter sailing backward over his chair. He lay very still.

"Get up, you fool!" the March Hare said.

But the Mad Hatter didn't stir.

"Is he OK?" Daphne asked.

Sabrina kneeled beside the Mad Hatter's body and nudged him gently. He was still breathing but unconscious.

"You knocked him out," Puck said, licking icing off his fingers. "Nice punch, too. For a rabbit."

The March Hare screeched in terror. "This is all your fault!"

"Our fault? You're the one serving up knuckle sandwiches," Daphne said. "Get ahold of yourself. We need to figure out what to do."

"Figure out what to do? There's nothing we can do, child. We're all doomed." The March Hare fled into the woods, shattering more teacups in his haste.

An unsettling feeling came over Sabrina as she watched the Hare run.

"Maybe we should get out of here, too," Sabrina said.

"Shouldn't we wait for the Mad Hatter to wake up?" Daphne said. "We can't just leave him lying there, can we?"

"And what about this cake?" Puck cried, gesturing to the table. "It's not going to eat itself."

"You both remember what the Editor said," Sabrina responded. "When his hungry little monsters show up—we're lunch. Besides, we need to keep following the yarn."

Sabrina had to physically yank Puck away from his beloved cake. He complained bitterly for several long minutes as they raced into the woods. Every time they nearly caught up with the ball of yarn, they encountered another bizarre character who wanted to talk. But the trio ran past each of them without a word. Sabrina preferred to keep her mouth shut than accidentally change *Alice's Adventures in Wonderland* any more than they already had. Eventually, they stopped to take a break at a small stream. The ball of yarn stopped rolling but bounced around, agitated and eager, like a soft, round bloodhound.

Puck lay down in the grass with his hands behind his head. "Ah, isn't this the life?"

Sabrina could hardly believe her ears. "You're enjoying this?"

"Aren't you? Jumping from one story to the next, playing around with history, changing people's destinies—this is first-rate mischief-making," Puck said.

"I will never understand you," she mumbled.

Puck laughed. "Isn't your heart beating extra fast? Don't you feel so alive? The last year of my life has been awesome! We've nearly died a dozen times already, and it's exhilarating! As much as I hate to admit it, you two have upped my street cred in the prankster community. We've busted a guy out of jail, broken into someone's house, killed dragons and giants, destroyed a bank and a school, changed the future, and started a civil war. You really should be proud of yourselves."

"I'll admit, it never gets boring," Daphne said with a sleepy laugh. She lay down and fell quickly asleep.

Sabrina was determined to keep moving, but they also needed rest. She'd let the little girl doze for an hour or so, and then they'd get going again.

"If you want to spill your guts about what's wrong, feel free, but don't expect a hug or a hanky," Puck said.

"What are you talking about? I'm fine," she said.

"You are smelly, annoying, and infuriating, but you are not fine. In fact, if I didn't know better, I would suspect a Levorian Ear Toad had burrowed into your brain. You haven't been yourself since we stepped into this book."

"Sorry to disappoint," Sabrina grumbled as she stared off into the forest.

"Oh, boy!" Puck said. "Listen, I gave you a chance, but if you don't—"

"I'm scared," she blurted, hardly believing she'd said it.

Puck grinned.

"Go ahead and laugh, dirtball, and I'll break your face." She took a deep breath. "I'm afraid of myself."

Puck arched an eyebrow. "Let's pretend I don't completely understand."

"I keep screwing up," Sabrina said. "In the last few weeks, I've helped a madman destroy our house and kidnap our brother, and I raced after him into this crazy book without a second thought. Now we're working for this Editor, who might be evil, and his little pink erasers keep trying to eat us."

Puck rolled his eyes. "I suppose you want a pity party."

Sabrina's face flushed with anger. "So I open up to you, and you make fun of me? You're a jerk."

"Duh!" Puck laughed, which made her even angrier. How could she ever have considered him a friend? Or had feelings for him? This was all just more proof that she couldn't trust her own instincts. At that moment, she decided she would never give this boy her heart. She didn't care what was supposed to happen in the future.

"I'm going for a walk," she snapped, and stormed off. She only made it several yards into the woods before Puck snatched her by the hand and pulled her roughly to the ground.

"Are you crazy?" Sabrina cried.

"Be quiet," he whispered, covering her mouth with his hand. "There are men coming. Lots of them."

Sabrina peered through the bushes and saw dozens of familiar figures rushing through the forest.

Sabrina gasped. "Card soldiers!"

If the storybook versions of card soldiers were as dangerous as their real-life counterparts, then the children needed to stay hidden. The two crouched, silent and still, while the strange army passed. Once they were gone, Sabrina and Puck crept out from their hiding spot and rushed back to the stream. Daphne was nowhere to be found.

"Do you think the soldiers took her?" Sabrina asked, panicked. She felt as if she might faint.

"Hey," a voice called from above. Sabrina and Puck looked up and found Daphne perched on a tree limb. "The army is everywhere. I can see hundreds of them from up here. We should keep moving."

With no time to waste, the children hurried through the woods. But they soon realized that something was following them. It wasn't a card soldier, because it traveled through the trees, jumping from one branch to the next, causing leaves and strange nuts to shower down on them. Puck's eyesight was much better than a human's, but even he couldn't spot their stalker.

"Just keep moving," Sabrina said, trying her best to sound calm around Daphne. "It's probably just a squirrel or something. When it gets bored with us, it will go find something else to chase."

Worrying about the mysterious creature had distracted the trio from paying attention to where the yarn was leading them, and, before long, they stumbled directly into a crowd of card soldiers as vicious as any Sabrina had ever seen. Their leader—the Nine of Diamonds—snatched the magic ball of yarn from the ground, eyed it closely, and then leveled his sword at Sabrina's heart.

"I suppose you three are the trespassers we've been hunting. The queen would like to make your acquaintance," the Nine of Diamonds said.

"Tell the queen thanks for the invitation, but we're a little busy," Sabrina said.

The Nine of Diamonds scowled and stepped closer until his sword was just inches from Sabrina's chest.

"Her Majesty demands your presence. You are creating mayhem in the story, and it must stop!" he shouted. The rest of the soldiers circled the trio, swords drawn.

"I suppose we can spare a few minutes for the queen," Puck said with a sheepish grin.

The soldiers marched the children through the forest until they came to a dirt road. There, they found a throng of horse-drawn coaches. Each horseman seemed more frantic than the last, clearly trying to get to his destination as quickly as possible.

"Out of the way!" they shouted at one another. "Royal business!"

The soldiers were unfazed by the chaos, and they led the trio into the heavy traffic. The group emerged on the other side, unscathed, none of the cards even mentioning the danger they'd all just passed through.

Soon, they reached a castle with two high towers. At the entrance stood a guard with the head of a frog. He wore white leggings, a red coat with tails, and a white powdered wig, but his face was a muddy green and slick with slime. His big, bulbous eyes spun in their sockets, but he wore a dignified, almost smug expression on his face.

"Hello, Sir Nine. I see you've captured the troublemakers," the frogman croaked.

"Of course I have," the Nine of Diamonds said. "Let us pass."

"I don't know," the frog said skeptically. "You could be an impostor."

"An impostor?! You've known me forever! I was at your wedding," Nine cried.

"Well, one can never be too careful," the frog croaked, eyeing the card soldier up and down. He then let out a loud harrumph. "Keep a close eye on your prisoners."

The Nine of Diamonds scowled and pushed past the amphibian guard. He led the children into a dark, damp tunnel beneath the castle.

They emerged into a beautiful garden. The lawn looked as if it had been trimmed by hand, and exotic flowers in bright, vibrant colors were planted everywhere. Fountains sprayed water high into the sky, creating shimmering rainbows. It was stunning, but Sabrina knew that not all was as it appeared. Nearby, a handful of soldiers busily painted white rosebuds red. When one of the soldiers splashed paint on another, they broke into an argument that nearly turned into a fistfight.

"The queen! The queen!" someone shouted, and a large procession marched into the garden. First came trumpeters, court jesters, jugglers, mimes, and balladeers. They were followed by more card soldiers, princes, and courtiers, then ten small children dressed in elaborate outfits embroidered with hearts. Finally, a white rabbit wearing a little red smoking jacket entered, shooing everyone out of his path.

"All eyes!" the rabbit sang. "The King and Queen of Hearts."

The Queen of Hearts entered to a shrill trumpet. At her side was a rather fidgety-looking man.

Sabrina scowled deeply. She knew the real-life queen quite well. She was the mayor of Ferryport Landing, and she had nearly destroyed the town with her bad decisions. She was also dedicated to making the Grimm family's lives miserable.

The king, however, Sabrina had never met. He looked just like the King of Hearts she saw on playing cards—complete with the strange beard that curled at the bottom. She had heard several conflicting stories about the queen's husband. Some said he'd decided to stay in Wonderland when Jacob and Wilhelm Grimm offered to take everyone to America. Others claimed the queen had murdered him in his sleep. Sabrina believed the latter to be true.

"Get to your places!" the Queen shrieked as she charged through the crowd, knocking over any soldiers and trumpeters who got in her way. "We're supposed to be playing croquet. We have to get this story back on track, now!"

Everyone dashed off in different directions and returned with a flock of pink flamingoes and several squirmy hedgehogs. The Queen took one of the lanky birds and held it upside down as if it were a croquet mallet. She placed the hedgehog on the ground and lined up the bird's beak with the hedgehog's behind. She swung wildly, missing her shot completely. Not that she could have hit the hedgehog, even with perfect aim. It wisely scurried off before it could be hurt or humiliated. But the Queen wasn't about to give up. She chased after the furry creature, swinging a dozen more times and knocking the daylights out of a few card guards. Soon, the playing field was a small but growing mountain of unconscious obstacles.

"Where are the interlopers?!" the queen shrieked.

The Nine of Diamonds shoved the children forward until they stood before the furious queen.

"Your Majesty," the Nine of Diamonds said, bowing deeply. "I have captured the three trespassers responsible for the alterations to our important tale. I hope you are most pleased."

The queen peered at the children as if she were eyeing a nest of cockroaches, then turned her attention back to the Nine of Diamonds. She flashed him a sickly sweet grin. "Well, they can't very well play the game without mallets and balls."

"Of—of course," the Nine of Diamonds stammered, leaping into action. A moment later he returned with more squawking flamingoes and agitated hedgehogs and shoved them into the children's hands. Sabrina's bird flapped furiously in an attempt to free itself, showering her in pink feathers. Daphne's hedgehog hissed and bit at her. When she set it on the ground, it promptly escaped. Puck's hedgehog crawled into his shirt, but he just giggled, delighted.

"I heard a rumor that you are from the real world," the queen said, aiming her flamingo at another spiny ball. She missed, but this time the force of the swing knocked her off her feet. Several soldiers helped her up and brushed her off with a great deal of gusto until she smacked each of them in the head.

"Children, I am talking to you," she snapped.

Sabrina could barely look at her. Somehow, the fictional version of the Queen of Hearts was even more troubling—and louder—than the real one.

Sabrina nodded quickly. "It's true. We're from the real world."

"Interesting . . ." the King of Hearts said.

The queen flashed him an angry expression. "What would you know?"

He muttered an apology before lowering his eyes.

"Why have you come here?" the queen demanded.

"We're searching for a boy called Pinocchio. He's traveling with several wooden marionettes that can walk and talk."

"And pinch," Daphne said, showing the purple bruise on the back of her arm.

"Yes, he came through here. My soldiers arrested him, but not before he caused a great deal of chaos."

"Since when is that a crime?" Puck asked.

As he ranted about the universal right to mischief and mayhem, Sabrina tried to process what the queen had just told her. *Does she really have Pinocchio in her custody? Could one of my family's bitterest enemies really be that helpful?*

"You have him?" she asked.

"Indeed, I do. The scamp ruined everything—changing dialogue, themes, and even characters. At this very moment, I am supposed to be having an argument about beheading the Cheshire Cat! As you can see, the cat is nowhere to be seen."

"I'm sure he's just running a bit late, Your Majesty," the White Rabbit said as he nervously eyed his golden pocket watch.

"Here's the troublemaker now," the King said, gesturing across the lawn.

Two card soldiers dragged Pinocchio into the garden. The guards had tied his hands behind his back, but he struggled to free himself nonetheless. A third guard followed, carrying a birdcage, and as they drew closer, Sabrina could see Pinocchio's marionettes locked inside it.

"You!" Pinocchio snarled as he glared at the children. "Why won't you let me be?"

"I don't know. Maybe it's because you betrayed us?" Sabrina said.

Daphne threw a punch into her open palm. "Let me at him."

"I didn't want to help the Master, but I had little choice. I have searched the world to find a cure for my affliction. I have spoken to wizards and witches and fairies and talking fish, but no one could help. Mirror offered me my only chance to fix the Blue Fairy's ill-conceived enchantment."

"Can anyone decipher what Mr. Fancy Pants is saying?" Puck asked.

"He's still complaining that he's never grown up," Sabrina explained.

"I've been this age for almost four thousand years," Puck said. "I kind of dig it."

"I suppose you'll be taking me back to the real world?" Pinocchio grumbled.

"Not at all. We're turning you over to the Editor. I don't know what he plans to do to you, but it's probably better than what I'd do," Sabrina threatened.

Four guards wearing black hoods approached. Sabrina noticed that they were Aces from all four suits: diamonds, hearts, spades, and clubs. Each carried a large, menacing ax. Behind them were more cards carrying tree stumps into the garden.

"What's all this?" Daphne asked, as the soldiers set down their tree stumps.

"This boy is a criminal. He has damaged the story, and he must be punished," the Queen barked. "Off with his head!"

One of the hooded soldiers forced Pinocchio's head onto the stump while another sharpened his ax.

"Whoa! Whoa! Whoa!" Sabrina cried. "You can't kill him!"

"We can't?" the King of Hearts asked. "We have the criminal. We have the stump. We even have the axes."

A guard waved his deadly blade in Sabrina's face. "See, they're very sharp!"

"The Editor hired us to track him down. We need to bring him back alive and well," Daphne said.

The Queen let out a frustrated harrumph. "I don't care what the Editor does. As the queen of Wonderland, I have the right to execute anyone I choose."

"Don't let them kill me," Pinocchio pleaded as he fought against the much-stronger men.

"If you kill the puppet, the Editor won't like it," Puck said.

"I'm not a puppet!" Pinocchio cried.

"Dear, dear, I think I understand what the children are saying," the king said, patting the queen on the back. "They're jealous that they aren't being executed."

"Very well," the queen said. "Off with all of their heads!"

Puck drew his sword, but the card soldiers snatched him from behind, knocking his weapon to the ground and tying his hands behind his back. Before the sisters could react, the card soldiers had them, too. They dragged the children to the stumps.

"I'm sure you understand," the queen said, "this is the only true deterrent to crime here in Wonderland. In the hundreds of beheadings I have ordered, only a handful of the criminals have become repeat offenders."

"On your command, Your Majesty," a hooded guard said.

Sabrina could not move. She could not speak. All she could do was look out of the corner of her eye at the sharp ax above her.

The queen cleared her throat. "Good sirs! Prepare your axes!"

5

S THE GUARDS LIFTED THEIR DEADLY BLADES, something fell from the trees above, landing in the crowd.

Sabrina craned her neck to get a better look and was surprised to find an enormous striped cat fighting the soldiers. The cat was nearly as big as she was. It swatted men left and right with its huge paws, and despite its fierce assault, a clever, almost happy smile stretched wide across its face.

Suddenly, the cat let out a high-pitched whistle, and more bizarre creatures rushed into the melee, including a giant puppy and a strange bird with an oversized beak.

The card soldiers were befuddled and overwhelmed. They jabbed their swords at the odd collection of animals. "Shoo! Shoo, you flea-bitten curses," they shouted.

The animals, however, held their ground. The puppy charged

at the men. The bird slammed its hard beak into them. At one point, even the White Rabbit joined their efforts, kicking and punching with all his might.

"What is the meaning of this?" the queen bellowed.

"We're busting out of this story!" the White Rabbit said, swinging his pocket watch threateningly. When the queen fell back in shock, the rabbit turned his attention to a hooded guard. "If you know what's good for you . . ."

The guard set down his ax and, along with the other executioners, fled.

The White Rabbit went to work untying Sabrina's hands. "Don't worry, child. I will free you," he said, hopping over to Daphne's side.

Unfortunately, he was too distracted to notice a card soldier rushing at him, sword in hand. The giant cat leaped into the soldier's path, saving the White Rabbit from certain death. The soldier swung his weapon at the feline's neck, but just before it landed, the cat's body vanished. Only his big, toothy grin remained, floating in the air.

"He's the Cheshire Cat," Daphne said, biting her palm.

The Cheshire Cat reappeared and then sunk his teeth into the card guard's leg. He dragged the soldier up a tree and impaled him on a sharp branch. Satisfied, the cat leaped from the tree and landed on all fours in front of the girls. He gave himself a good shake and, once again, smiled.

Meanwhile, the huge puppy scooped up several of the cards in his mouth and wrenched them around violently before dumping them back on the ground, dizzy and battered. The bird continued knocking guards out with a swift peck of his rock-hard beak.

The White Rabbit mostly just barked commands and warned the others of approaching attacks. Together, the oversized animals wiped out a majority of the queen's army. Those who were still able fled into the woods, along with the queen and the king and their flock of courtiers.

"Quick work, Dodo," the White Rabbit said proudly to the strange bird.

"Just as we planned," the Dodo replied.

"And not a scratch on us," the puppy said, before his attention turned to chasing his own tail.

The White Rabbit hopped over some of the unconscious soldiers, bouncing on one's head before he reached the children. He bowed deeply in respect. "Allow me to introduce myself."

"No need," Sabrina said, unable to hide her disgust. "We know who you are."

"I beg your pardon?"

"You're the White Rabbit," Sabrina said with a deep scowl. "And you're a member of the Scarlet Hand."

"The scarlet what?" the rabbit said.

"You're part of Mirror's army," Puck explained.

The rabbit turned to his friends, but they looked just as confused.

"I'm having some trouble understanding this conversation, children. I have never met any of you, ever. I'm sure I would remember. I don't know anyone called 'Mirror,' nor have I ever counted myself amongst any army—certainly not a scarlet one."

"He's not lying," Daphne said, frowning. "This isn't our White Rabbit. This is the one from Alice's story."

Puck rolled his eyes. "All this real-world and storybook-world talk is giving me a headache. The only question that matters is: Can I roast him for dinner or not?"

"No," Sabrina said. "Daphne's right. He's not a villain. None of them are."

"You can help us escape," the Dodo said cheerfully.

"We're not here for your prison break," Sabrina said. "We're here for Pinocchio. Where did he go?"

"Splinterface must have run off during the fight," Puck said.

"This Pinocchio is important to you?" the Dodo squawked.

"We can help you find him," the Cheshire Cat said. "Then, you can free us."

"Absolutely not!" Sabrina said. "You'll just slow us down."

"We saved your necks!" the White Rabbit argued. "If it weren't for us, your heads would be rolling around on the ground."

"I'm not sure we can take you out of the Book even if we wanted to," Daphne said. "You aren't real."

"How dare you! The second we leave the Book, we'll be as real as you," the puppy said.

"Trust us. You're better off in here," Sabrina said. "The town we live in is at war. Everything has been destroyed."

"You say all that like it's a bad thing," Puck said, surprised.

"Anything would be better than the endless tedium of being a character in a story that never ends," the Dodo said.

"What does *tedium* mean?" Daphne asked.

"Tedium is kind of a boredom due to repetition," said Sabrina.

"What does *repetition* mean?"

"Having to do something over and over again."

"It's like brushing your teeth or changing your underwear. Eventually you just have to give up," Puck said.

The Cheshire Cat ignored him and pressed on. "This story never ends. When it gets to the last page, we are all sent back to the beginning. Every day we say the same things, wear the same clothes, and a few of us meet the same untimely deaths. Imagine living a life where you cannot make your own decisions. Imagine being stuck in the same day, forever and ever."

"None of us volunteered to be in a living history book, and no one asks us if we are happy," the White Rabbit added. "The Editor is unsympathetic to our plight; thus, we have come to this drastic decision. The only way to escape our bondage is to escape the Book."

"That does sound horrible," Daphne said.

"Now don't start getting sensitive," Sabrina said to her. "I don't know the Editor well, but I don't think he'd approve of characters abandoning their stories, let alone the whole Book."

"Who put him in charge? He rules over us without mercy," the Dodo squawked. "Any little change in the story and we are devoured—our very existence is wiped clean."

"If things are so bad, why haven't you just gone through one of the red doors yourself?" Daphne asked.

"We've tried!" the puppy barked. "We can't open the doors. Only outsiders can do it."

Sabrina took a deep breath. She wished she could get away and analyze the problem. Being a Grimm meant never having time to think, and Sabrina knew what could come of quick, thoughtless decisions.

She hadn't been lying about the Editor; she suspected he would be furious if they helped characters escape. But she remembered something Mirror had said just after he revealed himself to be the Master. He said he felt like a prisoner, and no matter how nice the Grimms were to him, they couldn't give him his freedom. These four characters, strange as they were, wanted the same thing. How could she deny them? On the other hand, they were four more souls putting their lives in her hands. She couldn't be responsible for them, not with all the mistakes she had made in the last year. No! They couldn't come. What if something went wrong? It would be her fault. She opened her mouth to say as much, when Daphne interrupted her.

"All right, you can come with us, but let's get something straight," Daphne said to the animals. "We're not traipsing through these stories because they're fun. We're looking for Pinocchio. We can't have anyone slowing us down. If you fall behind, you're on your own. If you get hurt, we will leave you. If the Editor sends revisers, we can't stop to save you—so keep up!"

"Agreed," the White Rabbit said. "And in return, we will help you in your search. This Pinocchio you speak of sounds like a powerful foe. You may need all the help you can get."

"I don't know about this," Sabrina said.

"I will bite him!" the puppy said.

"Leave the biting to the experts," Puck said, baring his teeth.

"It's going to be all right, Sabrina," Daphne promised.

"Fine." Sabrina shrugged, giving in. "But it's not going to matter much if we don't find our way out of here. We need that ball of yarn."

The group searched the lawn for the Nine of Diamonds. They found him, still unconscious, surrounded by a mob of angry hedgehogs. The furry creatures allowed Sabrina to pass, and she snatched the yarn out of the soldier's hand. She felt the familiar tingle of magic and quickly tossed the ball to Daphne. The Cheshire Cat let out a loud squeal and leaped into the air, intercepting the ball. When he landed, he spat it out, then batted it around with his paws before Daphne snatched it away from him.

"Bad kitty," she chastised. "This is our only way out of here."

"Sorry, force of habit," said the cat sheepishly.

"I don't mean to be rude, but I believe it would be wise to get out of this particular story as soon as possible," the puppy said. "The Editor must have noticed the changes by now."

"Agreed!" the Dodo declared.

Daphne nodded and whispered into the ball before setting it on the ground. It rolled off into the woods.

"Intriguing," the White Rabbit mused.

"C'mon," Sabrina shouted, and they all dashed after the ball.

The group hurried along until they came to a red door standing in the forest. Daphne swung the door open, and a powerful blast of air escaped.

"This is it!" Sabrina cried.

Puck and Daphne were the first to step through the door.

"Be brave, friends," the White Rabbit said to his fellow rebels. He smoothed out his jacket and hopped across the threshold. Then, the huge puppy let out a cheerful howl and rushed in after him. Next, the Cheshire Cat bent down low and slinked through the portal.

"I never believed this day would come," the Dodo said as he stared at the open doorway.

"Save it for your diary, pal," Sabrina said. "We're in a hurry."

When the world came back into focus, the group found themselves in the thick undergrowth of a dark forest. They immediately spotted Pinocchio several yards away. He was bent over with hands on his knees, trying to catch his breath. When he spotted the group, he cursed and freed his wooden minions from their cage.

"Keep these fools away from me," Pinocchio ordered, and then dashed off deeper into the trees.

"Not the puppets again!" Sabrina whined.

"Don't worry, sweetie-pie," Puck said as the creatures raced toward them. "I won't let anyone put a finger on my bride-to-be."

The marionettes swarmed Puck. They climbed up his legs and back. They untied his shoelaces and yanked at his hair. When he finally managed to brush them off, they dove for Sabrina. She swatted at them, but every time she knocked one off, another took its place.

"You're doing a lousy job of protecting me, fairy boy," she cried.

With his sharp beak, the Dodo smashed the marionette that looked like Granny Relda and then attacked the one that resembled Veronica. Only the figures that looked like Daphne, Uncle Jake, and their father were left. The Cheshire Cat snatched them all up in his mouth while the puppy furiously dug a hole. The cat spat them into the hole, and the dog buried them just as quickly.

"I hate puppets!" Daphne cried.

"C'mon," Sabrina urged, and she charged into the woods after Pinocchio. Puck, Daphne, and the runaways from Wonderland followed.

They soon found him standing before a giant shoe. It was brown with a tarnished brass buckle and stood nearly twenty feet high. Set in the shoe's heel was a door decorated with a festive garland and a welcome mat. Sabrina watched Pinocchio rush through the door and slam it behind him.

"I guess we know what story this is," Sabrina said.

"Which one?" Puck asked.

"It's 'There Was an Old Woman Who Lived in a Shoe,'" Daphne said, and then bit down hard on her palm.

"Never heard of it," Puck said.

"Never heard of it!" Daphne exclaimed. "Everyone knows this story."

"I don't," Puck said. "If it's in a book, I'm blissfully unaware of its existence."

"It's a poem," Sabrina explained. "'There was an old woman who lived in a shoe. She had so many children, she didn't know what to do.'"

"That's it?" Puck said. "When does the monster come to eat the children?"

Daphne shook her head. "There is no monster."

"No dragon? No witch?"

"Nope," Sabrina said.

"Then what are we waiting for? Let's go inside and grab that pointy-nosed loser," Puck said. He threw the door open, only to be knocked over by a flood of filthy children. There were hundreds, maybe even thousands. It was hard to tell—they just kept coming and coming like the bubbles out of a shaken-up bottle of soda. Soon, everyone was in danger of being trampled. The Dodo grabbed the puppy and flew into the air, and the Cheshire Cat carried the White Rabbit up into a tall tree. Sabrina and Daphne dashed behind a boulder to stay safe.

A frail old woman appeared in the doorway. "Have fun!" she called to her children, who ran willy-nilly into the woods. "And don't be late for supper. We're having broth."

She spotted the group, eyed them angrily, then whispered, "Go away." She retreated into the house and slammed the door. Now that it was safe, the girls rushed to help Puck to his feet. The poor boy was covered in little shoe prints.

"I would have preferred a monster," Puck grumbled, slightly dazed. "Where's Pinocchio?"

A red door appeared across the clearing, and Sabrina watched

Pinocchio race toward it from the shoe. He quickly slipped through and slammed it behind him. The door dissolved before their eyes.

"He used those kids to distract us. The sneak!" Puck cried as he removed the wooden sword from his belt.

"I beg your forgiveness, but what do we do next?" the White Rabbit asked. "Shouldn't we go after the boy?"

Sabrina plopped down next to the shoe. She was tired and hungry and mad. She knew the ball of yarn would take them to another door if they asked, but what was the point? They had been in the Book of Everafter for days, and they were no closer to finding Mirror and their baby brother. Shouldn't that be their priority? What if chasing Pinocchio was just the Editor's way of distracting them? What if the Editor and Mirror were working together? It wasn't impossible—they'd been betrayed before. What should they do? And why was it always her job to decide?

"Next, we eat," Puck said, definitively. Sabrina wondered if his sudden leadership was an attempt to take the pressure off of her. But that didn't really make any sense. Puck was incapable of being so sensitive, and, besides, he was probably just hungry.

The rabbit and the cat grumbled but didn't say anything. The puppy sniffed the air and claimed he could lead them to food. Sabrina nodded. Maybe, with a little time and food, she could figure out what they should do next.

The puppy led them deeper into the woods until they came across an abandoned garden and a bank of walnut trees. Sabrina filled her pockets with all the walnuts, berries, carrots, and cucumbers she could carry and then suggested they set up camp near the shoe. She didn't want to be in the margins of the story any longer than necessary. Puck built a fire far bigger than they needed, but once it burned down to a reasonable size, the group sat and ate.

"Tell us of the real world," the Cheshire Cat begged.

"Yes," the puppy yipped. "What's it like?"

"Well, that depends on who you ask," Sabrina explained. "Most people live pretty uneventful lives."

"But not you?" the White Rabbit said.

Puck laughed.

"Nope! Our lives are nonstop excitement," Daphne said. "We're always fighting monsters and saving the world."

"Monsters!" the White Rabbit exclaimed.

"Just in our hometown," Sabrina said. "The rest of the world, for the most part, is happily dull. But unfortunately, even after you escape this book, you'll be stuck in Ferryport Landing. There's a spell that traps Everafters within the town limits."

The animals shared uncomfortable looks and fell quiet for a moment.

"I'll happily trade this prison for another," the Dodo said. "At least there is no one watching your every move and making sure you do as you're told."

"You mentioned that I was different from your White Rabbit?" the rabbit asked.

"Yeah, he's a jerk," Puck said, his face smeared with juice from the berries. "Evil, too. Not that being evil necessarily makes you a bad person or anything."

The White Rabbit gasped.

"He's a member of a very mean group called the Scarlet Hand. They're trying to take over the world," Daphne explained.

"This boy you're chasing, Pinocchio . . . Is he their leader?" the Cheshire Cat asked.

"No, but he's a member of the Hand," Sabrina explained. "The leader's name is Mirror. He's traveling through the Book, too. He was our friend, or at least we thought he was, but he betrayed us and kidnapped our little brother. He wants to steal our brother's body for himself so that he can be a real person."

"Well, we will help you stop him," the Dodo crowed.

The puppy growled. "It is the very least we can do in return for your help."

The characters kept asking questions about the real world. They were fascinated with little things like cars and phones and indoor plumbing, though the White Rabbit couldn't accept that, in the real world, most animals didn't speak.

The refugees from Wonderland daydreamed about the lives they intended to build when they finally escaped the Book of Everafter. Now that they were free from their story, they wanted to celebrate with songs and tales of their own epic escape. But Sabrina didn't feel much like a party. As the night went on, she developed a sharp headache. Daphne seemed to sense her pain. The little girl took Sabrina by the hand and led her away from camp.

"What have you've done with my sister?" she asked.

Sabrina shook her head. "I don't understand."

"You're not really Sabrina Grimm," Daphne said. "The real Sabrina never doubts her decisions."

Sabrina sighed.

"Normally, I find it annoying," Daphne continued. "I mean, you always do what you want and almost never ask me what I think, and that makes me really mad sometimes."

"I'm afraid I'll make the wrong choices."

Daphne was quiet. "'Cause you trusted Mirror and he turned out to be the bad guy?"

Sabrina was surprised by her sister's insight. It was another sign that Daphne wasn't such a little girl anymore. "How did you guess?"

"Uh, because I trusted him, too," Daphne said. "He was like an uncle to me. When he turned out to be the Master, I couldn't believe I hadn't figured it out myself. Then, I looked back on all our time with him and started seeing the clues: the two faces he showed—one for the reflection and one for the Hall of Wonders—and how whenever we discussed a plan around him, the bad guys always seemed to know, and all those mirrors we found around town—Nottingham and Heart had one, and there was one in Oz's workshop. There was even one in Rumpelstiltskin's office. Jack probably had one, too. That was how Mirror talked to his evil army. Why didn't I see it before? I'm a Grimm. I'm a detective. I have mad fighting skills and can zap someone with a magic wand like nobody's business . . . but he totally fooled me."

"So why aren't you panicking like me?" Sabrina asked. "After the people you trust betray you, how do you know which decisions are right?"

"You don't," Daphne said as she munched on the last of her walnuts.

"What?"

"No one knows if their decisions are right until after they make them. You can only do the best you can," Daphne said. "Listen, you're being way too hard on yourself. Mirror's been plotting this forever. He's a magical creature with magical abilities. It's not like you got fooled by some random moron."

"I guess," Sabrina said. Daphne was making total sense, but it still didn't make her feel much better.

"Plus, Mirror wanted his freedom so badly that he was willing to do terrible things to get it. It's impossible to prepare for something like that, right? He's been trapped in that mirror for hundreds of years. He's had owners who were cruel to him. He's been treated like property. I can't blame him for wanting out."

"You're quite the empath," Sabrina said.

"Pretend I'm not a dictionary and I don't know what that word means."

"It means that you understand other people's problems," Sabrina said.

"Well, that only goes so far. When you mess with my family, I stop caring about your problems. Mirror hurt you and me and everyone we love. He's going down. I guess that's how I know my decisions are right or wrong. Protecting my family will always be right."

Sabrina blinked. "When did you get so wise?"

"Remember all those old Westerns Mom used to watch on TV? All the cowboys talk like that," Daphne said matter-of-factly.

The fire had burned down to embers when Sabrina and Daphne returned to camp.

"What now?" the Cheshire Cat asked.

Daphne flashed Sabrina a knowing look and a smile. It was a relief for Sabrina to have her sister's approval.

"We can follow the ball of yarn into the woods," Sabrina said.

"But I don't think that's the best idea. There's something in the margins."

"Yes, the ghost." The puppy whined, afraid.

"So, instead, I think we should give this story an ending and hope a new door appears."

"That makes sense," Daphne agreed. "This little old lady lives in a shoe. She's got so many kids, she doesn't know what to do. How do we end it?"

"I think the old woman probably needs a little help organizing," Sabrina said. "Puck, take the others and find the children. Get them back to the shoe as quickly as you can. Daphne and I will get everything ready."

Puck and the escapees from Wonderland raced off. It wasn't long before they returned with all the children. It probably helped speed things up when Puck transformed into a pterodactyl and frightened them into running for their lives. When the children were gathered, Sabrina called for their attention.

"Listen up," Sabrina announced. "You kids have had it too easy. Your mother feeds you, clothes you, washes your laundry, and keeps your rooms clean. She's exhausted. She's inside taking a long-overdue nap, so we're going to get this shoe in tip-top shape. If your name starts with the letter *A*, raise your hand."

A dozen children raised their hands.

"You are going to mow the yard, rake the leaves, and clean out the gutters," Daphne said.

The children whined.

"No whining!" Sabrina snapped. "If your name starts with *B*, you're on laundry duty. There's a pile of dirty socks in there as high as a mountain. They need to be washed, dried, folded, and put away."

"If your name starts with a *C*, you're on dishes," Daphne added. "Wash them, dry them, and put them away. And remember, don't overload the dishwasher!"

The chores went on all the way to Zed, Zelma, Ziggy, and the rest of the *Z*s. The children washed windows, swept the walkway, bagged grass clippings, and beat the dust out of rugs. When the little old woman came outside hours later, there were tears in her eyes.

"Thank you! Thank you!" she cried.

"Don't mention it," Daphne said as a red door materialized.

"Look! It worked! Let's get going before it disappears," Sabrina said.

Daphne opened the door and whispered something into the magic yarn. It hopped out of her hand and into the void. Puck followed, then Daphne. Sabrina gestured for the animals, and together they stepped into the unknown.

The group stood at the bottom of a rocky hill topped with a majestic castle. It overlooked a green valley and a churning river. Unlike the old, crumbling castles Sabrina had seen in her father's travel magazines, this one was pristine—almost as if it were brand-new. Its walls were made of gleaming white marble, and a proud orange flag featuring a fierce black griffin flapped in the wind. Before Sabrina could ask her sister which story they were in, a loud explosion shook the ground, and the blue sky turned an angry red.

"Dear, dear," the Dodo said as it hid behind Daphne. "We've just stepped into a war zone."

Another explosion echoed across the valley, and a moment later one of the castle's towers toppled over and crashed against the rocks. The next thing Sabrina knew, three knights in full armor came charging straight toward them. Sabrina stepped out of the way, only to fall to the ground with a thud. She hadn't realized she was also wearing a heavy suit of armor.

Puck pulled her to her feet.

"Sir Galahad! Sir Bedivere!" one of the knights shouted to the girls. "The Editor has sent a sorcerer to put down our rebellion. Merlin is fighting him off, but he is very powerful. He has attacked the castle, but we will not cease fighting for our cause. Freedom will be ours!"

"Cause?" Sabrina asked. "What cause?"

"To escape the Book, of course," the second knight said proudly. "We are members of the Character Liberation Army."

The third knight looked as if he were ready to add more to the conversation, when he rubbed his eyes and stared at the group. "What manner of creatures are you?"

"It's complicated," Sabrina said to the knight. "What story is this?"

The third knight gasped. "You've come from another story? Then the rumors are true! Our fight has merit."

"Can it be?" the first knight cried.

"Beware, they may be in league with the Editor!" the second knight shouted. At this, all three knights drew their swords.

"All right, you walking tin cans," Puck said. "Don't do something you'll regret."

Sabrina raised her hands to calm everyone down. "We're not in league with anyone. We're looking for someone—a little boy."

There was another explosion, and one of the castle walls crumbled to dust.

"If the villain fighting Merlin inside is a little boy, the world is certainly doomed," the third knight said.

"This sorcerer . . . Can you take us to him?" Sabrina asked.

"Are you daft? It would be foolish to return to the castle," the second knight cried.

"If you won't take us, we'll go on our own." Daphne took slow, deliberate steps forward in her suit of armor. It wasn't long before she tipped forward and landed face-first. "Stupid armor! Whose idea was it to wear two hundred pounds of metal into battle? A duckling could kill me right now."

Sabrina and Puck helped the little girl to her feet. The knights dismounted and helped remove some of Daphne and Sabrina's heavier pieces of armor. Soon, the girls were moving a bit more freely.

"You really plan to go into that fight?" one of the knights, who had introduced himself as Sir Port, asked. "You're fools, but the rules of chivalry will not allow us to turn our backs on you. We will be your escorts."

The Dodo cleared his throat. "Um, let's not be too hasty. Perhaps we should wait here until the fighting is over."

"Remember the deal, bird," Sabrina said. "We won't come back for you."

"I must object," the White Rabbit interjected as he polished his monocle. "The two of you have taken on roles in this story. Any number of horrible things could happen to you. Perhaps it would be wise to entrust your magic yarn to us. Just in case."

Sabrina eyed the group suspiciously. "The yarn is ours, buster."

The White Rabbit threw up his paws. "Of course! Of course! Just a suggestion."

Despite the others' objections, Sabrina charged forward. She, Puck, Daphne, and the three knights climbed up the steep hill and crossed a wide drawbridge over a foul-smelling moat.

They entered the castle courtyard through a grand arch. There was smoke everywhere. Sabrina saw a panicked crowd made up of knights, ladies-in-waiting, and court jesters rushing about in an attempt to avoid the battle. Sabrina could feel the familiar tingle of enchantments all around her. Clearly, someone was wielding some very powerful magic.

They pushed their way through the crowd and eventually found the battle itself. Sabrina saw two figures circling each other. Their hands were alight with fire, and their eyes burned with magic. Every time one of them made the slightest movement, the air crackled with energy.

"Someone should stop this," said a tall, handsome man with flowing black hair.

When Sabrina looked up into his face, she immediately recognized him as Sir Lancelot, a member of King Arthur's court and one of Ferryport Landing's volunteer firefighters. Granny Relda had recently purchased a Firefighters of Ferryport Landing calendar, and whenever she took a peek at it, she blushed as red as a stoplight.

Lancelot's familiar face told Sabrina which story they had entered—the tale of King Arthur and his Knights of the Round Table.

"This cursed interloper stepped through an enchanted doorway in the midst of our castle," Lancelot explained. "Myself and a battalion of noble knights came to the defense of Camelot, but we were soon overwhelmed by the villain's magic. We called to Merlin for help, due to his experience with the black arts, and he is locked in an ungodly battle with the villain."

"What did he say?" Daphne asked.

Sabrina shrugged and turned to take in the battle once more. She could make out Merlin, old and feeble, and expected to see him fighting Pinocchio. But, instead, she spotted a short, balding man in a black suit.

"Daphne, it's Mirror!" she exclaimed. "We found him!"

"Then where is Rodney?" Daphne asked.

"Rodney?"

"Fine! Where's our baby brother?" Daphne cried.

"The cherub you speak of is there, with the queen," Lancelot said, pointing across the courtyard to a slender, pale woman with long blond hair. She wore an eggshell-white silk dress embellished with tiny, delicate flowers. In her arms was a small, red-haired toddler.

"C'mon, let's get him," Puck said, and the trio shoved their way through the crowd. Soon, they were standing before the queen and the baby boy.

"Guinevere!" Daphne called.

The woman was indeed King Arthur's famous wife. Sabrina had met the woman a few times in Ferryport Landing and had found her to be sweet and polite. She was a stark contrast to her usually hotheaded husband, Arthur.

"Do I know you, child?"

"The real you does," Daphne said. "We're from outside the Book."

Guinevere's eyes grew wide. "Then word of our rebellion has reached far and wide. Have you come to help liberate us?"

"Not exactly," Sabrina said. "The little boy you're holding is our brother."

"He demanded I guard the child with my life," the queen said, pointing to Mirror. Lightning bolts erupted from his hands and eyes. "I fear he means it."

"He belongs with us," Sabrina said, taking the boy into her arms. She looked into his face. She could feel he was family, from the shape of his eyes to the smell of his skin. He was as familiar to her as Daphne.

"Hello? I'm your sister, Sabrina," she said to him.

"We should go while baldy is distracted," Puck said. "Plus, that kid needs a diaper change."

"I think that smell is you," Sabrina said. "But you're right. Let's get out of here."

"What about Pinocchio?" Daphne asked. "We made a deal with the Editor."

Sabrina scanned the crowd, but there was no sign of Pinocchio. "I know a deal's a deal, Daphne, but let's take our brother and get out of here while we still can. Mirror isn't going to be happy when he discovers we've caught up with them."

For once, Daphne didn't argue. She whispered her instructions into the ball of yarn, and it rolled into the crowd. The trio chased it as quickly as they could. They were jostled and shoved mercilessly, but Sabrina didn't mind. Her heart was brimming with joy. The baby in her arms completed her family. Finally, she had done something right. Daphne ran alongside with happy tears in her eyes. Even Puck, who despised the joy of others, had a grin on his face.

Just as they caught up with the yarn, there was an explosion that knocked them off their feet. Sabrina checked to see if her brother was hurt, but besides a few startled cries he was perfectly fine. Puck helped the girls up, and they scanned the eerily quiet crowd.

"What just happened?" he asked.

"He killed Merlin," a stranger said as a troubled murmur rose up from the crowd. "I can't believe it. He actually killed him. That is definitely not supposed to happen in this story."

A familiar voice bellowed, "WHERE IS THE BOY?"

"Daddy!" the child in Sabrina's arms cried.

"Daddy?" Daphne repeated. "Mirror isn't your daddy."

An invisible force created a path through the crowd from Mirror to the children. Sabrina saw Merlin lying on his back. Mirror stood over him, his face boiling with anger, his eyes fixed on Sabrina. She quaked with fear.

Daphne was just as terrified. Even Puck's bravado was gone, but he stepped forward nonetheless. The girls had seen him fight giants, dragons, and Jabberwockies—all with a mischievous grin on his face. But this time he was deadly serious.

"I won't let you take him again," Puck warned.

Mirror's face softened, and he laughed. "Well, look what we have here! The sisters Grimm and their sidekick—Puck, the wonder fairy." Mirror marched toward the trio, his hands still crackling with energy. "I underestimated you three. I really didn't think you'd catch up to me in the Book, but here you are. And look, Puck is ready for a fight. You realize you've bitten off more than you can chew—right, Trickster King?"

"You're no more than a reflection. If I were you, I'd leave this story before I break you into a million pieces," Puck threatened.

"You are as stubborn as you are pungent, boy," Mirror said, raising his hands. Fire sprang from his fingers. "Give me the child, or you are going to make one very smelly corpse."

6

IRROR BLASTED ENERGY FROM HIS FINGER-
tips, hitting Puck squarely in the chest. The
fairy let out a pained scream and flew backward
several yards. A moment later, he slowly stood up and smiled
weakly. "Your joy buzzer doesn't hurt that much."

Mirror shocked Puck again, with similar results.

Sabrina rushed to Puck's side. "Stop it!" she demanded.

"Honestly, children," Mirror said, pacing, "I wish you could
see my side of the story. I've been trapped in the Hall of Wonders
for hundreds of years, always the slave of whoever owned me.
And when I saw a chance to take my freedom, I took it. Any one
of you would do the same."

"I wouldn't kidnap anyone," snapped Sabrina. "I wouldn't
steal an innocent child from his family."

"I get no joy from this, Sabrina," said Mirror. "If I could do it another way, I would, but your family is the only human family I've had direct contact with in decades."

"So we were easy prey?" Daphne asked.

Mirror frowned and lowered his hands. The power in them faded, as did his anger. "I genuinely cared about you, all of you."

"Don't lie to us!" Sabrina shrieked.

A panicked scream rose up from the crowd.

"They're coming!" someone cried. "Run for your lives!"

The crowd stampeded through the courtyard as a few desperate knights struggled to raise the drawbridge. Sabrina spotted King Arthur, his magical sword Excalibur raised and ready.

"Who's coming?" Sabrina asked, keeping one eye on Mirror.

"The Editor hath sent his filthy creatures upon us," Arthur said.

"Revisers!" Mirror cried. Sabrina was surprised to see him so afraid. Apparently, there were things in the Book that could hurt him.

The drawbridge came crashing down with a horrible crunch just as a wave of revisers scurried into the court. The refugees from Wonderland were with them, running for their lives. When they spotted Sabrina, Daphne, and Puck, they rejoined the trio, cowering and trembling in fear.

Arthur and his knights rushed forward to fight the revisers, slashing desperately with their swords. One reviser latched on to Sabrina, but she managed to pull it off and toss it away. Sometime during the struggle, Mirror disappeared into the crowd.

"We better get out of here," Puck said as he got to his feet.

"There goes the ball of yarn." Daphne pointed to the magic ball racing through the chaos.

"Let's go!" Sabrina, holding her brother tightly in her arms, led the group after the yarn. Together, they weaved a haphazard path through the courtyard, circling columns and doubling back around fountains. Eventually, the yarn led them into the castle itself.

"Please pick up the pace!" the Dodo squawked. "The revisers are nipping at our heels."

The monsters were gaining on them and devouring everything in their way. Everything they ate was replaced with blank white nothingness.

The yarn led the group up a flight of stairs and down a long passageway. At the end, they found the ball jumping and rolling against a huge wooden door. Daphne tried the knob, but it was locked.

"Open it," the puppy whined.

"I can't! We don't have a key!" Daphne explained.

"I can get it open, but you must agree to take me with you," a voice said from the shadows. It was Pinocchio.

"You!" Sabrina cried.

"Do we have a deal?"

The revisers were gaining on them. "Do it." Daphne nodded.

Pinocchio took a pin from his pocket and went to work picking the lock.

"Please hurry," the White Rabbit whimpered.

"Be quiet," Pinocchio snapped. He kept at the lock until there was a loud click. He pushed the door open, and the group clambered inside, slamming the door behind them.

"Just a little trick I learned while living on the streets of Italy," Pinocchio bragged.

Sabrina ignored him. Waiting in the room was a second door, this one red and magical. Mirror stood blocking it.

"You set us up," Sabrina accused Pinocchio.

"I swear I didn't know he was in here," Pinocchio said.

"If you were still a puppet, your nose would be growing so fast right now!" Daphne cried.

"Give me the child, Sabrina," Mirror demanded, interrupting the bickering.

Sabrina shook her head and struggled to calm her squirming brother. "He belongs with us."

Mirror's face turned purple with rage, and his eyes grew dark. "That door will not slow down the revisers. Once they arrive, they will devour this room and everyone in it, including your brother."

"Then get out of the way," Puck said.

"Your dispute does not involve us. Step aside and let us pass," the White Rabbit demanded.

"Yes, we're just trying to leave," the puppy said.

"I'll let everyone through this door if you give me the boy," Mirror said.

"Hand him over, girls," the Cheshire Cat ordered, stepping forward as if to take the baby from Sabrina. "What good is there in letting us all die?"

Puck drew his sword. "The first one of you who tries is going to be my new coat."

A reviser took a large bite of the wooden door and then squeezed through the hole and into the room. Its sharp little teeth gnashed wildly. It sprang for the Dodo. The bird pounded at it with its huge beak, but the reviser was relentless. It clamped its teeth onto the bird as two more revisers pushed their way into the room. Soon, all three were attacking the Dodo, erasing him bite by bite.

"Give him to me, Sabrina," Mirror said with open arms. "Your friends from Wonderland will be remade by the Editor. We're from the real world. We don't get a second chance. They'll kill us all."

"Daddy!" the little boy cried. He squirmed in Sabrina's arms, reaching for Mirror.

"Give him to Mirror," Daphne said.

Sabrina turned to her, shocked that her sister was willing to surrender.

"There's no other way out," Daphne continued. "And we'll have another chance to stop him."

Daphne was right. Reluctantly, Sabrina handed her brother over to Mirror. He opened the door and stepped into the angry wind and was gone.

"A very responsible choice," the White Rabbit said with a nod.

If Sabrina could have killed someone with a single look, the White Rabbit would have died on the spot. "Get through the door, you cowards!" she shouted.

The crowd pushed past her and fled through the door.

"You're sticking with me, toothpick," Puck said to Pinocchio, snatching him up by the collar. Pinocchio grabbed the fairy god-mother wand and flicked it at Puck. Thankfully, the blast missed Puck's leg, but it hit the ball of magic yarn instead. Smoke bil-lowed out of it. Pinocchio squirmed free and jumped through the portal before anyone could stop him.

Daphne reached down for the ball. "Uh-oh."

"Just go!" Sabrina said as the tears welling in her eyes spilled over. She followed the others through the door as the revisers screeched in anger.

Sabrina found herself inside a tiny coach packed tight with squirm-ing children. The group's sudden appearance triggered a massive groan from the crowd, who jostled each other roughly.

"Sabrina!" Daphne called from somewhere in the pack.

"I'm here," Sabrina said.

"Where are we?" the Cheshire Cat demanded.

"I don't know. Does anyone see Mirror?" Daphne asked.

There was no reply. Sabrina wondered if the Book of Everafter had dropped him into a different story, or a different part of this one.

"I see puppet boy," Puck said. "He's up front."

Sabrina pushed forward to look through the coach's tiny window. Sitting on the driver's seat was a short, tubby man who steered a team of donkeys. Beside him was Pinocchio.

"What story are we in?" Sabrina called out to him.

"Mine," Pinocchio said, beaming.

"Uh-oh," Daphne said.

"We have to get out of here," Sabrina said, spinning around to look for a way out of the coach.

But the crowd was too close, it was too hot, and she felt nauseated. She pulled at the bars that covered the windows and tried to shove her way through the crowd. She was trapped! She tried to take a deep breath, but there wasn't enough air, and then everything went black.

When she woke, Sabrina was lying on a cold cobblestone street. Her sister and a crowd of other concerned faces were gathered around her.

"Give her some air," the Cheshire Cat shouted.

"What happened?" She tried sitting up, but she felt so weak, she decided against it.

"You fainted," Daphne said. "I was really worried."

"Where are we?" she asked.

Daphne pointed down the road toward a town square lined with multicolored houses. The street was littered with discarded toys. Everywhere Sabrina looked, there were children running and playing without a care in the world. The biggest house on the street was under attack by an army of kids dressed in tinfoil armor. A banner reading WELCOME TO TOYLAND hung over the square. Other signs, fastened to that one, read TOYS ARE GRATE! NO MORE SKOOLS! DOWN WITH RITT MATTICK!

"We have to catch Pinocchio," said Sabrina. "When we turn him over to the Editor, he'll lead us to Mirror."

"Just rest," Daphne said.

Sabrina forced herself to her feet. "We can't. There's no time."

"Well, we've got a big problem," Daphne said. She took out the ball of yarn and whispered Pinocchio's name into it. It fell to the ground, popping and fizzing, but it wouldn't roll forward. "That magic wand blast fried it."

"Then we'll have to do this the old-fashioned way." Sabrina frowned. "We'll split up. White Rabbit, puppy, and Cheshire Cat—you're in one group. My sister and Puck and I will stick together."

"I must protest this plan," the White Rabbit said. "What if we do not find one another again? Any number of things could happen while we are here. One of us could become injured—or we could get lost. We would be trapped here."

"I really don't care, Rabbit! Finding our brother is more important than your stupid escape."

Daphne raised her hands to calm everyone down. "Rabbit, you've got a pocket watch. Meet us back here in an hour. And everyone else, do yourself a favor and don't play with any of the kids in the town. Playing is a bad, bad thing."

"That's insane," Puck said. "You're not making any sense."

"Playing is going to turn every kid on this island into a donkey," Daphne explained, pointing to those pulling the coach. "The driver will sell them all to farms, where they will be worked to death, or worse."

"What's worse?" Sabrina asked.

"They skin you and use it to make drums," said a boy as he approached from the town.

"Drums!" the White Rabbit cried in horror.

"How do you know that, anyway?" the Cheshire Cat purred.

"I'm Lampwick, Pinocchio's best friend. Just a friendly warning. Now, I gotta go." The boy rushed off to join the other children but stopped when Sabrina called him back.

"Wait! Where are you going?" Sabrina said. "If you know how this ends, why not turn around and go home?"

The boy shook his head. "The Editor would not approve."

"Then join us," the puppy offered. "We're traveling through the stories. Soon we'll find a door to the real world, and we'll escape for good. You could be free."

Lampwick smiled and shook his head. "And then what? I have an important role to play in Pinocchio's character development. When he witnesses my death as a broken-down farm animal, it has a profound effect on him. Without me, his efforts to become a good boy could be compromised. Even though I play a small part in his life, it's an essential one."

"You're a fool!" the White Rabbit said.

"In any good story, the hero must encounter tragedy in order to grow. My death makes my pal a better person. I'm arguably the most important character in his story. How can I walk away from that?"

And with that, the boy disappeared into the throng of kids.

"Nonsense," the White Rabbit grumbled.

"We're wasting time. Come on! Let's find Pinocchio and get out of here," Sabrina said.

The two groups split up and went their separate ways, promising to meet back in an hour. Sabrina, Puck, and Daphne traipsed down an alley, careful to avoid the children and their dangerous games. Two boys were playing "catch the firecracker." Others were having a pitchfork-throwing contest.

"I shouldn't have given him back to Mirror," Sabrina said,

thinking about her brother. The guilt she felt was overwhelming, and she blinked back tears.

"I told you to! We had no choice," Daphne said.

Sabrina ignored her. "What if we don't get him back?"

"We will get him back," Puck said. "I'll make sure of it."

The boy's face was determined, and every hint of sarcasm and silliness was gone from his voice.

"You're not alone here, Sabrina," Daphne added. "We're a team, and we all would have done the same thing. Besides, you're forgetting something. Mirror's story is off-limits. The Editor said Mirror can't get into it, so whatever he has planned for Carmine won't happen."

"Carmine?" Puck said.

Daphne rolled her eyes. "Fine! Let's just call him Baby X! Are you two happy?"

Sabrina couldn't help but laugh. "Baby X is worse than Carmine."

"I kind of like it," Puck said.

The trio laughed together and, for a moment, Sabrina believed that things might turn out all right.

"OK, enough with the boohoo faces," Puck said. "There will be plenty of time for regret when we get married."

Sabrina rolled her eyes. "Daphne, you've read this story, right? What do we need to know?"

"Well, eventually Pinocchio turns into a donkey, and he gets sold to the circus. Then, his owner tries to drown him in the ocean—"

"What kind of children's story is this?" Sabrina interrupted, horrified.

"An awesome one," Puck said, suddenly interested. "Are there explosions? Please tell me there's a vampire attack!"

"Sorry, no vampires. A fisherman catches him, I think. He might live with the Blue Fairy for a while, and then he gets eaten by a shark, maybe? There are lots of twists and turns."

"The shark is even better than a vampire attack—unless it's a vampire shark. That would be pretty cool," Puck said with a grin.

Daphne was still trying to puzzle out the order of the story's events when the puppy raced to join them.

"We found him! C'mon!"

The children followed the puppy through the senseless maze of Toyland's streets. Once, they had to circle back to find another path when they ran into a group of children gleefully trying to shatter the windows in a large church. The stained-glass shards came down like razor-sharp rainbows, and there was no safe way to pass. Another street was crowded with a jousting tournament. Two children rode donkeys at each other and took turns trying to knock their opponent off with pillows. A little boy ran through the onlookers with a can of green paint, splashing people and giggling like an idiot.

Finally, they came upon a filthy tent where the Cheshire Cat and the White Rabbit waited, as well as the driver of the coach. He was standing next to a trembling donkey.

"He's selling the animals," the Cheshire Cat said.

"Disgusting practice," the White Rabbit complained.

"Has Pinocchio already turned into a donkey?" Sabrina asked.

"He couldn't have. The story said he was in Toyland for weeks before he changed," Daphne explained.

The Cheshire Cat motioned to a dark corner of the tent. "He's over there hiding in the shadows."

"He must be trying to hurry the story along," Daphne said. "Can he do that?"

"It's his story," Puck replied with a shrug.

The coach driver led the donkey outside and displayed it before the waiting crowd. "How much will you give me for this fine, strong animal?" he asked.

"I'll take him for twenty-five nickels," a man in the crowd said. "I can use his skin for a drum I have at home that needs repairing."

The donkey brayed and whimpered until the driver hit him with a whip.

"Does he dance?" another man shouted.

"Pardon?"

A man dressed in a long coat, white pants, and black boots stepped forward. "Does he dance? My circus is in need of an act. If he can dance, I'll pay fifty nickels."

"You're a ringmaster, I see. You could teach him to dance for your circus."

"NO! He must dance now. I won't pay for a donkey that doesn't dance."

Suddenly, Pinocchio stepped out of the shadows. "He dances," he said. "Like a prima ballerina. I've seen him myself."

The coach driver and the ringmaster were confused. "Listen, boy. Don't change the story," the driver snapped. "Go sit down before you cause trouble."

"This is my story, and I can do what I want," Pinocchio said. "Ringmaster, buy the donkey, and I will accompany you to your circus."

"What is going on here? Does the Editor know about this?" another man in the crowd asked.

Pinocchio took out the magic wand. With a flick of his wrist, a blue flame shot from the tip. It sent a wave of surprised cries through the tent.

"The Editor cannot stop me, and neither can you," said Pinocchio threateningly. "Now, if you have eaten up enough of the oxygen with your stupid questions, can we get on with it?"

The coach driver nodded. "Congratulations, ringmaster. You just purchased a donkey."

The crowd leaped to their feet, arguing about the sudden change in the story and the repercussions that were sure to follow. In all the excitement, Sabrina lost sight of Pinocchio. One moment he was standing at the center of everything; the next he was gone.

"He's getting away. Find him!" Sabrina shouted, and they all raced away from the tent. They dashed down the streets, asking everyone they met if they'd seen Pinocchio. But nearly all of the children laughed in their faces or pelted them with crab apples.

"Little kids are jerks," Sabrina complained.

"Um, hello?" Daphne said with mock offense.

"Sorry," Sabrina said. "Where should we look for him next?"

"In the story, he's the one who gets sold to the circus. The Blue Fairy shows up at one of the shows," Daphne said. "I guess that's where he would go next, to try to find her. It's his chance to get her to fix the spell that keeps him a boy."

"And how, exactly, are we going to find a traveling circus?" the White Rabbit demanded.

"I don't know, but we better do it quickly," Daphne said. "Everyone who stays here ends up eating hay and swatting at flies with their tails."

For once, no one argued, and the group hurried to exit through the town gate.

"Hey, where are you going?" a girl called as they passed.

"We're running away to join the circus," Sabrina replied.

"It's dangerous to go into the parts of the story that aren't written. The margins are full of ghosties."

"What's inside the margins isn't all that great, either," Sabrina said, and the group continued on.

A few steps outside town, Sabrina spotted a sign pointing them toward the circus. But it didn't tell them how far away it was. The group walked for the better part of a day until they decided to make a camp for the night.

Puck suggested they hunt in the woods for dinner, but the White Rabbit insisted they refrain, vowing to defend his brothers or sisters. The Cheshire Cat and the puppy went off in search of water and fruit. Daphne collected some wood to build a campfire.

Sabrina wanted to help, but she felt beaten down. Her feet were throbbing, and her head felt like it'd been hit with a wrecking ball. She closed her eyes, hoping to block out the pain, and soon fell asleep.

When she awoke, she found a wild boar roasting above a crackling fire.

"Where did that come from?" she asked, rubbing her eyes to make sure she wasn't seeing things.

"I got skills, Grimm," Puck bragged.

"Not really," Daphne corrected. "He was chasing it, and it fell off a cliff."

Puck shrugged. "That was my plan all along."

When the food was ready, Sabrina ate like a starving coyote. Even with her belly full, she didn't feel that much better. In fact, she was still terribly exhausted. She hobbled away to a patch of soft grass and asked Daphne to join her.

"I need to rest," she said apologetically. "You're in charge."

Sabrina didn't hear Daphne's response because, a moment later, she fell into a deep, dark, dreamless sleep. Sometime in the night, she was awoken by a terrible blow to her rib cage. She leaped up and scrambled backward, only to find that the others were sound asleep and there was no one else around. She stood catching her breath in the cool night air, while the campfire burned down to embers. Her body ached from the attack, and when she pulled up her shirt, she found the beginnings of a bruise. *It wasn't a dream. Something attacked me, but what?*

Sabrina searched the ground, wondering if something had fallen from the tree above her, but there was nothing. She peered into the woods—maybe it had been a wild animal that darted off when she woke? She saw something move in the trees to her left. It vanished and thcn appeared again on her right. She squinted in the starlight, trying make out what it was, when it raced toward her at breakneck speed. Soon, it was standing over her. It wasn't a creature, exactly, but rather the faint notion of something. It was as large as a man but mostly invisible, made from the swirling dust and dirt of the forest floor.

It laughed, deep and angry.

"What are you?" Sabrina asked.

"I am doom," it croaked. When she blinked, it vanished.

"You've been quiet all morning," Daphne told Sabrina.

"I just want to find Pinocchio as soon as we can," Sabrina lied. She didn't want to frighten her sister with thoughts of ghosts. There were too many other things to worry about.

The Cheshire Cat caught some unidentifiable fish in the stream. They cooked them over a fresh fire, had some breakfast, and then picked up their search for Pinocchio. Another long day of walking led them to another town. It was so small, they would have missed it if not for the huge sign tacked to a tree.

GRAND GALA SHOW

This evening

**WITNESS THE TROUPE'S USUAL AMAZING LEAPS &
FEATS PERFORMED BY ALL ITS ARTISTS**

& all its horses, mares and stallions alike,

plus

appearing for the first time

the famous

DONKEY PINOCCHIO

also known as

THE STAR OF THE DANCE

The theater will be as bright as day

Puck stopped an old man who was hobbling down the road. The man pointed him to the theater at the other end of the town, but not before he gave him a good swat with his cane. He apparently objected to Puck calling him "gramps."

They dashed to the box office, but with no money they were forced to barter for tickets. After much begging, Sabrina finally convinced the White Rabbit to part with his gold pocket watch. It got them all front-row seats, plus a few nickels to spend at the local grocer. Unfortunately, there wasn't enough money in the world to shut the Rabbit up about "the great indignity" he'd suffered. He claimed he felt naked without his timepiece and kept fussing about being late for important dates.

While they waited for the show to begin, Sabrina, Puck, and Daphne searched the crowd for signs of Pinocchio or the Blue Fairy.

"Are you sure the Blue Fairy shows up in this part of the story?" Sabrina asked her sister.

Daphne nodded. "Pretty sure."

"I have a few ideas I'd like to run past you about how we plan to stop ol' splinter bottom," Puck said. "First, I'd like to clobber him with a chair. It happens all the time on television and seems fairly effective. Plus, it will make me very happy."

"At this point I think we should do whatever it takes," Sabrina said.

"Thanks, honey bunny," he said, giving her an exaggerated wink.

"If you call me that again, I'm going to hit *you* with a chair," she grumbled.

Bright brass horns introduced the show, and the audience applauded with enthusiasm. The ringmaster from the donkey auction came out and bowed deeply to the crowd, but there was something wrong with his face. In the blazing theater lights, he looked bewildered, almost frightened. He reminded Sabrina of Mikey Beiterman, a budding actor in her second-grade class back in Manhattan. During a school production of *Little Shop of Horrors*, he forgot his lines. He was so embarrassed, he burst into tears and ran backstage, refusing to return for the rest of the play. The ringmaster had the same look of panic.

"Ladies and gentlemen, I'm afraid the act advertised tonight featuring Pinocchio the dancing donkey has been canceled. Instead, I offer you the amazing Russian Stallion Brigade."

Several white stallions entered the tent, led by beautiful twin ladies who trotted the horses in a circle.

The audience murmured, and a little boy stood up and cried, "That's not how the story goes. Bring out Pinocchio!"

The audience cheered their approval.

"I can't," the ringmaster said. "Pinocchio is . . . he's changing the story. He refuses to transform into a donkey, and when I insisted, he threatened me."

"He'll bring the revisers down on us all!" a woman shrieked.

"Where is he?" Sabrina asked, jumping to her feet.

"There he is!" a man shouted, pointing to the seats in the upper deck. There, Pinocchio was pulling a woman with bright blue hair out of her seat and out of the tent, while shaking his magic wand at her.

"He's got the Blue Fairy!" Daphne yelled, and the group rushed from the tent and into the street to confront him.

"Stay out of this," Pinocchio snapped.

"We're not going to let you do this, puppet boy," Daphne said.

"I wasn't a puppet! I was a marionette!"

"Pinocchio! What on earth has gotten into you? I'm like your mother in this story," the Blue Fairy said.

"My mother? Well, Mom, you're the worst! I suffered greatly, and you didn't lift a finger to help. I was turned into a donkey. I spent a week in the belly of a shark. Two murderers hung me from a tree outside your house. A man tried to drown me. What did you do, O Mother dear? Nothing! You're the most powerful Everafter of them all, and you did nothing!"

"I understand why you're angry," the fairy said, "but I'm not the real Blue Fairy, just a storybook portrait of her. You can't get any revenge on me, because I haven't done anything. Perhaps you should go find the real Blue Fairy."

"No! She hides her identity, and even if I found her, she'd

pull the same nonsense again. Her magic always has a catch. The Book of Everafter is my only hope of getting the spell right, and you're going to help me. I want to be a man."

Puck charged forward, but Pinocchio turned his wand on him. "You stay back, you filthy street urchin. I'll shoot you with this, I swear. I went easy on you before, fairy."

Sabrina and Daphne joined Puck, as did the White Rabbit, puppy, and Cheshire Cat. "There's a bunch of us and only one of you. You could manage to get off one shot, maybe two, but you can't hit us all."

"I warned you!" the boy said, flicking the wand. A bolt of energy burst from it and hit the puppy squarely in the head. When the smoke dissipated, a pineapple sat in the puppy's place.

"Get him!" Puck shouted, and the group rushed forward. More explosions came from the wand, but someone snatched it from Pinocchio's grip, and he was soon defenseless. He screamed, cursed, and threatened, but when the dust settled, Pinocchio was on the ground with his hands secured behind his back, Puck sitting atop him.

"How dare you!" Pinocchio shouted. "I have a right to live like a normal person. I have a right to grow up!"

"I might have thought the same thing, once. But you betrayed us. Whatever the Editor chooses to do with you is exactly what you deserve," Sabrina said. "Hey, Editor! We've got him!"

A red door materialized from thin air and swung wide open. The Editor stood in a brilliant light.

"Good news, boss. We caught the puppet," Daphne said.

The Editor eyed Pinocchio, then turned his attention to the White Rabbit and the Cheshire Cat. His face puckered in disgust.

"These characters do not belong in this story," he said coolly.

"They're with us," Sabrina said. "We've been—"

"They will have to go back!"

Suddenly, the White Rabbit snatched a thick branch from the ground. The Cheshire Cat showed his teeth and growled.

"You're not going to torment us anymore!" the White Rabbit shouted. He swung the branch, murder in his eyes.

"Stay away from me!" the Editor demanded, stepping back through the doorway to avoid being hit.

"Girls, shield your eyes," the Cheshire Cat commanded. "This is going to get messy."

7

THE GROUP FORCED THEIR WAY INTO THE library, sending revisers darting off in every direction. They scurried up the bookshelves, climbing higher and higher. The Editor knocked over his leather chair in an effort to get away.

"Stop fighting!" Sabrina shouted to the characters from Wonderland.

"What is this place?" the White Rabbit asked, hopping around in an agitated manner.

"This is his library. It's where he devises his plots against us!" the Cheshire Cat said.

The Editor scowled. "I do no such thing. I have no interest in plotting against you."

"He lies!" the White Rabbit cried.

"I said, leave him alone!" Sabrina demanded.

"Don't pretend to be concerned for me, traitors," the Editor snapped. "You brought your revolutionaries to my doorstep."

"What? We're not part of any revolution," Sabrina said.

The Editor turned his attention to the White Rabbit. "So, rabbit, you are not content to be a character in a book anymore?"

"Not content in the least."

He turned to the Cheshire Cat. "And you feel the same way? I suppose you think you deserve freedom?"

"Indeed," the Cheshire Cat said. "We want out of this book. We're tired of doing the same things over and over again. We want to live in the real world, where we can do and say whatever we please without fear of being revised."

The Editor laughed. What started out as a small chuckle escalated until tears were streaming down his face.

"What's so funny?" the White Rabbit asked.

"You are! You think you're real!" the Editor said, wiping the tears from his eyes. "You aren't any more real than I am—you're nothing but fuzzy memories of things that happened hundreds of years ago. You are recollections put down in words and sentences and brought to life by a little bit of magic. You are portraits—and oftentimes, failed portraits—of actual someones. You're not even as real as the shadows of the creatures you represent."

Pinocchio pulled away from Puck and stepped toward the Editor. "I am not with these fools. I am from the real world, and I came here to alter my story. I am shocked and dismayed that you violated your role as guardian and sent the Grimms to prevent me from achieving my goal. I must protest! I demand you return me to my story so I can make changes."

"You are correct. I have changed the rules—or, rather, changed them back. This book was created to give your kind a stroll down memory lane. It was never intended as a way to change history. Do you know what has to be done when you change something? The entire story has to be rewritten in its original form, down to even the tiniest detail." The Editor straightened his tweed suit jacket. "The stories just can't take the changes. They're not built for reimagining. The Book of Everafter is closed for business."

"Enough!" the White Rabbit shouted. "We have no interest in changing who we are. All we want is out! We know you can open a door to the real world."

"It's a simple request. Just do it, and we won't have to get rough," the Cheshire Cat demanded.

"Do you think I respond to threats? I am the Editor. I control this book and everything in it."

"You are mistaken, sir," the White Rabbit said. "We have minds and desires, and we will not be enslaved another day."

"I hoped you would listen to reason, but you have left me with only one choice." The Editor sighed and then raised his hands above his head. There was a loud scurrying sound, as if all the world's cockroaches were marching toward them. Sabrina looked at the ceiling and saw the revisers crawling down the bookshelves. Some of them leaped and landed directly atop the characters from

Wonderland, digging their angry teeth into arms and legs. Both were soon erased by the pink creatures. A moment later, they circled Sabrina, Daphne, Puck, and Pinocchio.

"Call them off, Editor. We did what you wanted!" Sabrina demanded.

"I told you before that I can't always control them," the man said. "You have meddled too much. But I do thank you for bringing me the trespasser. When all of you are revised, I will no longer fear for the stability of the Book."

Sabrina scanned the room and spotted the red door they'd used to get into the library.

"Run!" she shouted, and the four children stomped their way through the monsters. Sabrina opened the door and felt a damp, chilly wind on her face.

"Where does it go?" Puck asked as he pulled a reviser from his leg and threw it across the room.

"Does it matter?" Daphne asked, then leaped through the doorway. Puck and Pinocchio followed.

Sabrina looked back and caught the Editor's eye. "This wasn't our fault."

"You marched an army into my sanctuary. They threatened to kill me if I didn't give them what they wanted. You're on your own, Grimm!"

"You promised to take us to Mirror!"

His face was as cold as stone.

Defeated, she backed into the doorway. The last thing she saw were the revisers charging toward her.

Sabrina sat astride a horse in the middle of a country road. Nearby, an old wooden bridge spanned a bubbling brook. The moon's reflection danced on the water.

"Where are we?" Pinocchio grumbled. He, Daphne, and Puck stood next to her.

"I don't know," Daphne said. "But it seems familiar."

Sabrina felt the same way. She scanned the woods, which were made up of oaks and cedars. These trees were just like the ones in Ferryport Landing. It smelled like home, too. Still, like all the other stories, everything seemed slightly out of focus.

"Could we be back home?" she wondered aloud.

"Not unless you dress like that all the time," Puck snickered.

Sabrina was wearing short black pants, a heavy wool cloak, a shirt with a stiff white collar, and a wig.

The horse let out a scared whinny and reared back. Sabrina grabbed for the reins and struggled to stay in the saddle. The horse stomped around, snorting and whimpering.

"What's wrong with this thing?" Sabrina asked.

"Maybe he got a whiff of you," Puck teased.

"He sees something," Daphne said, pointing into the woods. "Something is there, and it's frightening him. Do you think it could be the ghost we keep seeing in the margins?"

"There are no such things as ghosts," Pinocchio said.

"No such thing as talking puppets, either," Sabrina said.

Pinocchio sneered.

"There!" Daphne cried. A figure atop a black horse waited on the other side of the bridge. Sabrina couldn't make out his features, but his body looked misshapen.

"Who are you?" Sabrina cried out, but the figure did not reply.

"It's never good when they don't talk," Puck said.

"Maybe he's shy?" Daphne offered.

Suddenly the horse and its rider charged the bridge, coming to a halt halfway across. The sudden movement startled Sabrina's horse, and she had to use all her strength and balance to get him back under control.

"Listen, man. You are freaking out my horse, so cut it out with all the creepy stuff," Sabrina said angrily.

The figure, once again, did not respond.

"I'm warning you, pal. You do that again, and I'm going to knock your block off!"

The figure edged his horse closer and stopped in a beam of moonlight, which revealed why he seemed so oddly shaped. He was headless.

The horse was just as strange, with eyes flickering with flame and smoke blasting out of its nostrils. A chill ran through Sabrina. She had come face-to-face with lots of monsters, but all of them had had heads.

"This is 'The Legend of Sleepy Hollow,'" Daphne said as the rider drew a long silver sword. "That's why everything seems familiar. Sleepy Hollow is in upstate New York. That dude is the Headless Horseman."

"Get on the horse," Sabrina demanded, reaching down for her sister's hand.

Puck hoisted Daphne up onto the horse. "I'm assuming the plan is to run," he said.

"Absolutely," Sabrina said, clenching the reins tightly in her hands. "Any pointers on riding a horse?"

"It's easy once you get them started," the fairy said, and then smacked the horse on the behind so hard, it sounded like a thunderclap. The horse took off like a shot. Sabrina and Daphne bounced around on its back like microwave popcorn but held on with all their strength. All the while, the headless horseman chased them.

"They should put seat belts on this thing," Daphne cried. "If we don't slow down, we're going to fall off."

"But if we slow down, he's going to catch us!" Sabrina shouted. Just then, Puck zipped by with his wings flapping furiously. Pinocchio hung from his arms, complaining about Puck's "manhandling."

"I have a thousand questions for that guy," Puck said. "Like, how do you pick your nose if you don't have a head? How do you belch? Did it hurt when he lost his head? And what happened to the head?"

"Uh, it's right there!" Daphne cried as she pointed back to the monster.

Sabrina craned her neck and saw the Headless Horseman removing a ghostly pale head from a saddlebag. It was wrapped in filthy rags.

"We have to start carrying a camera with us," Puck said. "No one is ever going to believe this. Plus, I can put the photos in my scrapbook."

"Scrapbook?" Sabrina asked.

Puck blushed. "My . . . uh . . . evil scrapbook."

"Sabrina, stop!" Daphne said, and Sabrina pulled hard on the reins. Their horse skidded to a stop on the pebbled path. A second later, the Headless Horseman's head sailed past them, landing hard on the ground and rolling down an embankment.

"Did he just throw his head at us?" Puck cried. "That is totally awesome. Wait a minute. I just got a great idea for centerpieces at our wedding reception . . ."

The Horseman stopped in the road for a moment as if confused, then steered his horse down the embankment after his head.

"Shouldn't we use this opportunity to put some distance between us and the evil man with no head?" Pinocchio asked. "What if he comes back?"

"I've read the story," Daphne said. "We're at the end. He was supposed to throw his head at Ichabod Crane. I guess that's who Sabrina's supposed to be."

"And that's it? That's how the story ends?" Sabrina asked.

"Yep," Daphne said. "He's probably waiting for everything to start over."

"If it's over, then where's the door?" Puck asked.

Sabrina was afraid of the answer. Maybe the Editor wasn't letting one appear for them. Maybe he was trapping them in the story until his revisers arrived. Without the magic ball of yarn, there was no way to know for sure. There could be a door waiting for them in the woods, but there was no way to find it.

"This is all very tedious," Pinocchio complained. "Set me down and come back for me when you find the door."

Puck dropped him unceremoniously, and the boy fell hard on his rump.

"We have no idea where to look," Sabrina said.

"Isn't that just great!" Pinocchio cried, rubbing his sore behind.

"Well, we need to look for it, but first I've got to find somewhere to go to the bathroom," Daphne admitted.

"Daphne, it's too dangerous," Sabrina said. "You'll have to hold it."

"If you don't let me go, something bad is going to happen," the little girl said. She started a little dance, shuffling her feet back and forth.

Sabrina sighed. "Don't go far, and come—"

Before Sabrina could finish, Daphne darted off like a road-runner.

Meanwhile, Puck took the liberty of tying Pinocchio to a tree with duct tape. Sabrina couldn't get him to explain why he had a roll of duct tape but then realized the boy's pockets were probably full of emergency prank supplies.

Puck laughed at the little traitor. "Honestly, I don't know if I can get you free. That's a lot of tape. We might have to leave you here."

"You wouldn't dare!" the boy seethed.

"You don't know him at all," Sabrina said.

"So," Puck said, turning to Sabrina. "I'm glad you're feeling better. When you fainted back in Toyland, I thought you were dead."

"You wish." Sabrina rolled her eyes.

Puck shook his head. "No way! You can't die. I've already registered for wedding gifts. If you croak, I'll never get that mayonnaise cannon."

Sabrina was about to ask which store sold a mayonnaise cannon, then realized she probably didn't want to know. It would just lead to more jokes about weddings and marriage. Puck was really beating this one into the ground, though Sabrina had to admit, she didn't think it had ever been very funny.

"You're not failing, you know," Puck said suddenly.

"Huh?"

"I know you're afraid. All your confidence is gone, and you hesitate every time you have to make a decision now. I thought you should know that I think you're doing a pretty good job. I mean, you've kept most of us alive. Sure, all those weird animals are dead, but they were super annoying."

"I was wrong about Mirror," Sabrina said quietly.

"We were all wrong about Mirror," he said.

"And then I gambled with my baby brother's life. I turned the Editor against us. I got us hopelessly lost more than once. I don't even know how to get out of the Book. I wasted time and energy tracking down that idiot," she rambled, pointing at Pinocchio.

"Hey! You're aware that I can hear you, correct?" the little boy complained.

"Well, wrong turns happen when you're the hero," said Puck.

"Huh?"

"Listen, we've been running through stories for days now, and I've noticed something about all of them. The hero always has a terrible time—tiger attacks, melting witches, people throwing their heads at you. It seems like everywhere we go, there's an obstacle in our way, but that's what is supposed to happen. Remember what that weird Lampwick kid said when we were in splinterface's story? The hero faces challenges so they can overcome them."

"My life is not a story," Sabrina said.

"Everyone's life is a story. But it's one they write themselves. You'll see. When we get married, you'll even get a happily ever after." Puck chuckled.

"Don't make me feel worse," Sabrina groaned.

Puck frowned. Sabrina wondered if all the boy's teasing about marrying her was actually teasing. *Is he serious?*

"Well, being a hero hasn't been so great for me, either. I should be planning pranks like what kind of gunk to pour over your head, but instead I'm considering how my actions might affect you!" he complained. "I used to be a villain. I was the Trickster King, the shaman of stupidity, the Dalai Lama of dumb jokes. Now look at me! I'm Mr. Sensitive. Well, I'm done with it."

"Puck, I didn't mean—" she started.

"Sabrina!" Daphne cried as she raced into the clearing.

Sabrina and Puck rushed to meet her. "What's wrong? Were you attacked?"

"What? No," Daphne said. "I think I know how to get a door to appear for us. We'll do what we did in 'There Was an Old Woman Who Lived in a Shoe.' We'll give the story a new ending."

"How?"

"We have to give the horseman his head."

"You're insane. We should stay as far away from that devil as possible," Pinocchio cried, pulling at the tape that bound him.

"We don't have any choice," Daphne said to him. "And we can't do it at all without you."

"Me?" Pinocchio looked alarmed. "What does this have to do with me?"

8

I T TOOK A WHILE TO CUT THE DUCT TAPE AWAY FROM
Pinocchio. When he was free, the children walked back to the
road. It was late now, and the air was crisp and chilly. Sabrina
could see a puff of mist whenever she exhaled.

"What do you want me to do?" Pinocchio asked, clearly put
out by the request.

"All you have to do is stand in the road and taunt the Horseman," Sabrina said.

"So I'm the bait?"

"No, you're just very good at being annoying," Daphne said.

"How dare you!"

"Oh, and hold this," Puck said. From underneath his hoodie
he removed a melon-shaped object wrapped in old rags. It smelled
foul.

"What's this?" he asked, taking it from Puck and examining it
closely.

"It's a head."

Pinocchio let out a scream and dropped the head. Puck quickly scooped it off the ground and forced it back into his hands. "Careful! This is valuable."

"You had his head the whole time?" Sabrina asked.

Puck nodded.

"Why?" Daphne asked, her eyes as big as saucers.

"It's a souvenir," Puck said. "I was thinking I'd put it on the mantel above the old lady's fireplace when we got home."

"It's someone's head!" Sabrina exclaimed.

"It's a conversation piece," Puck corrected her. "And I want it back when we're done!"

"What are you three going to do?" Pinocchio asked as he held the head as far away from his body as possible.

"We're going to hide," Sabrina said, and the trio scuttled off into the brush.

"How long do I have to wait here?" Pinocchio demanded.

"According to the story, the Horseman is obsessed with getting his head back. He should be here pretty soon," Daphne promised.

After several moments, the Horseman had still not arrived, and Pinocchio was growing impatient.

"Someone else needs to take a turn with this thing," he complained.

"Make some noise. Be obnoxious. Tease him!" Sabrina called.

Pinocchio frowned and lifted the head over his own. "Hey!

Horseman! I got your head. Nah-nah-nah!" He let his arms drop and turned to the children. "Happy?"

"You are worthless," Sabrina said, marching out into the road. She snatched the head from the boy and waved it around. "Hey, Horseman! You want your head? Too bad! It's mine now!"

Pinocchio growled. "Sorry if I don't have a lot of experience taunting people with their own body parts."

"You don't have a lot of experience doing anything for any-one else," Sabrina said. "For someone who claims to be an adult trapped in a little boy's body, you sure act like a baby."

"You insolent brat!" Pinocchio said. "If I were big enough, I'd take you down."

"I'd like to see you try," Sabrina said, clenching her fists.

"Hey, you two! Shut up. He's coming!" Daphne said.

Daphne was right. Sabrina could hear the pounding of hooves on the road. Then the dark, terrifying figure appeared. His sil-ver sword flashed in the moonlight, and smoke billowed from his horse's nose.

"Where's the door?" Sabrina cried.

"It should appear any second," Daphne replied.

"You better be right," Sabrina said. "Or you're going to inherit my hat collection!"

Pinocchio sprinted away in fear, leaving Sabrina alone. She tucked the head under her arm and chased after him, but after only a few steps she heard Puck's voice shout, "No!"

Sabrina turned to find the boy fairy in the road with his wooden sword in his hand. The dark horse reeled back, and the Headless Horseman lost his balance. He fell off and slammed into the ground with a thud. Then he got to his feet and raced toward Puck.

"Give him his head!" Puck called.

Sabrina tossed it to the Headless Horseman, and a red door in the road materialized next to her. When Daphne opened it, all four children darted through.

Sabrina stood in an arid desert, blinking into the brutal sun. She took a deep breath, and sand burned her throat.

"At least it's not a forest," Pinocchio said. "All these woodland stories are doing a number on my allergies."

"Where do you think we are?" Daphne asked.

"Not a clue," Sabrina said as she rolled up her sleeves.

"Maybe someone in there can tell us," Puck said, pointing behind the group to a marble staircase that led down into the earth.

"Here we go again," Sabrina said with a sigh.

The children scrambled down the stairs and into a lush, subterranean garden. Despite the lack of sunlight, fruit trees and flowers grew. A stream fed the greenery, and little birds fluttered from one branch to the next. Four glass vases overflowed with golden coins.

Sabrina looked at her sister, hoping she had figured out which story this was, but Daphne just shrugged.

At the end of the garden, they found a second flight of stairs that led even farther underground. There was little light, so the group clung to one another and groped blindly along the walls.

They soon came to a set of double doors that glinted gold in the darkness. Puck pushed them open to reveal a room overflowing with jewels and precious metals. Several torches illuminated the room, and the treasure sparkled brightly, nearly blinding Sabrina. In the center of it all, she could make out two figures. The first was a short, balding man. The second was a toddler.

"So you found me," Mirror said. The youngest member of the Grimm family sat at his feet, burbling happily.

Daphne rushed toward the boy, but Mirror's eyes ignited with magic, and Sabrina pulled her back.

"You didn't think we'd give up, did you?" Sabrina said.

"No, I suppose I didn't. Funny, it was a quality I once admired in you. Now it's sort of annoying," Mirror said.

"It didn't have to be like this," Sabrina said. "You're family. We could have found another way to get you what you wanted. You didn't even give us a chance."

Mirror shook his head. "I've asked others before you. Eventually, I got tired of counting on the kindness of others."

He leaned down and snatched a golden lamp from a pile of treasure. It was nothing special compared to everything surrounding it, but Mirror was clearly in awe.

Sabrina suddenly understood where the Book of Everafter had placed them. They were in *One Thousand and One Nights*. They

were traipsing around in Aladdin's story, and Mirror was holding more than just a lamp.

"Don't do this," she begged.

Mirror frowned. "The Editor won't let me into my story. It was the only chance I had to change my life, and he's locked the door. If this lamp is as good as the real thing, it's my key."

Mirror polished the lamp against his suit jacket, and a strange energy filled the air. Pressure pushed against Sabrina's eardrums, and a loud pounding rocked the cavern. A purple mist seeped from the lamp. It swirled in loops higher and higher above them until it formed a single, massive being—half man and half smoke. It stood nearly twenty feet tall, and its arms were thick with muscles. It looked down on them and snarled, "Who summons me?"

Mirror raised his hand. "That would be me."

"As is my obligation, I must grant you three wishes, but I have been trapped in this lamp for eons. You would be most kind to use one of your wishes to grant me my freedom."

"You'll get no such satisfaction from me, genie," Mirror said.

The genie roared with rage, and the temple's walls shook. Dust fell from the ceiling, and Sabrina worried the whole thing might cave in on them.

"Simmer down," Mirror said, seemingly unfazed. "I released you from the lamp. I am your master. We've got some work to do, and I suggest we do it before the Editor and his revisers arrive. Do you possess the same power as your real-life counterpart?"

"I do, but once I am revised, your wishes will be, too," the genie snarled. "You will only benefit from them for a brief time."

"I only need a few minutes. Let's get started," Mirror said. "I wish this child and I were in the story of 'Snow White and the Seven Dwarfs.'"

"That story is off-limits," the genie said. "There are barriers to entrance."

"Did you not just say you are powerful? You can raise the dead, change the course of rivers, and make the world bow at your master's feet. Use your powers to remove the barrier," Mirror demanded. "Do as I command."

"Very well, but you have been warned." The genie clapped his hands and created a mighty explosion. Mirror and the baby Grimm began to shimmer as if thousands of lightning bugs were crawling under their skin. They grew so bright, Sabrina had to shield her eyes. When the light faded, Mirror and her brother were gone.

"Send us, too," Daphne begged.

The genie shook his head. "I cannot. Mirror is my master. I am his to command."

"But he didn't use all his wishes!" Sabrina said. "Give them to us."

"They are his wishes. I cannot offer them to you."

Sabrina was so angry, she kicked a crown resting by her foot. "We're stuck. He knew this would happen. That's why he didn't use the other two wishes."

"We'll just have to find another door," Daphne said.

"We don't have time. He's in his story right now!" Sabrina cried. "He won. He's going to steal our brother's body for his own."

She leaned against a column and slid to the floor, remembering the bleak future she and her sister had seen when they fell into the time tear. Mirror ruined the world—dragons hunted humans, monsters roamed free, and the world cowered beneath the flag of the Scarlet Hand. All of their efforts were for nothing. The girls could not save the world.

"What do we do?" Daphne asked.

"Nothing. It's over," Sabrina said.

Suddenly, a blast of wind blew her hair back. A door appeared, and through it stepped three figures engulfed in a blinding light.

"Why the long face, *liebling*?" Granny Relda asked. Sabrina's mother, Veronica, and her father, Henry, were standing beside her. The girls threw their arms around their family and squeezed tightly.

"How did you find us?" Daphne asked.

"There are detailed instructions in the journals, girls," their grandmother said.

"We're going to have to have a very long talk, young ladies, about rushing headfirst into danger without your family," Henry scolded.

"Oh, Henry. There's time for that later," Veronica said. "Are you kids OK? Have you been hurt? Why did you come into this book in the first place?"

"Mirror is the Master," Sabrina told them. "He jumped into it, and we chased after him."

Granny Relda swayed on the spot and grabbed Henry for support. "That can't be. Our Mirror?"

"He's been behind everything. Jack, Rumpelstiltskin, the Mad Hatter, Oz, Mrs. Heart, Nottingham—they've been taking all their orders from him," Sabrina said.

"And he's not finished with us," Daphne said. "His next plan involves our brother."

"Brother?!" Henry cried.

Veronica took her husband's hands. "Henry, I don't know how to tell you this," Veronica said. "The night we were abducted, I had an important announcement."

"Veronica?"

"I was pregnant."

Henry blinked. Then he blinked again. "A baby?"

Veronica nodded. "He was born while we were sleeping."

She explained to Henry about the magic Mirror had used on her to deliver the child and how she herself didn't know the baby was born until the night the Scarlet Hand attacked the fort. She apologized for not telling him right away, but she wanted to be sure she had all of the correct information before filling him in.

"Mirror built a nursery hidden in the Hall of Wonders. He's been taking care of Baby X ever since," Daphne said.

"Baby X?"

"I've been trying to name him, but nobody likes my ideas," Daphne grumbled.

"I liked Oohg," Puck said. "Though I think Puck is a wonderful name for a boy."

"We have a son . . ." Henry whispered, teary-eyed.

Daphne's expression turned serious. "Yes, and Mirror has him. He's gone into his own story, and if he succeeds in changing it, he's going to take over our brother's body. He wants to be a human, not an Everafter. He doesn't want to be trapped in the Hall of Wonders anymore."

"He'll have all his powers, and as a human child he'll be able to step through the barrier into the real world," Sabrina explained.

"And you helped?" Granny asked Pinocchio.

Pinocchio's face turned red with shame. "He promised to help me grow up."

"We need to go to his story, Relda," Veronica said.

"That's the problem," Sabrina said. "We can't. There's this guy—he calls himself the Editor—and he won't let us. He says 'Snow White and the Seven Dwarfs' is off-limits."

"And he has monsters that tried to eat us," Daphne said.

"The Editor?" Henry asked.

"Yes, the guardian of the Book," Granny said as she removed an old leather-bound journal from her bag. The cover read *The*

Fairy-Tale Accounts by Trixie Grimm. "When the town wanted to create this book, Trixie offered to help. She worried that the magic inside it might be used in troubling ways, so she became a sort of guardian, keeping an eye on the visitors and lending a hand to people who got into jams. She had an assistant created to help her. She called him the Editor.

"But something must have gone wrong. Without warning or explanation, Trixie locked the Book up in the Hall of Wonders. She wouldn't let anyone near it." Granny flipped through the journal to a section that had been torn out. Several pages were missing. "Even her accounts from that time are gone. It was like she was trying to hide something, even from our family."

"Or maybe she was trying to protect us," Henry said.

"Perhaps. Unfortunately, Trixie is no longer with us—God rest her soul—so she can't tell us herself. However, the Editor will know what happened. I think it's time we paid him a visit."

"That's not going to be so easy," Daphne said. "The only way to get into his library is if he opens the door himself."

"And we kind of irked him," Puck admitted. "He's very sensitive."

"Trixie mentioned in her notes that he was persnickety," Granny said, flipping through the book. "That's why she left us a key to his library."

Granny removed the key from a pocket on the inside cover of the journal, leaned forward as if she were standing in front of a door, and inserted the key into air. Suddenly, a red door materialized around the key. She turned the key and opened the door. Sabrina could hear the familiar sound of a fireplace crackling.

"He's got monsters, Granny," Daphne warned.

"I think we'll be all right," she said, giving the little girl a wink.

"If I had a wish, I would set you free," Daphne said, turning to the genie.

The creature nodded respectfully and watched the family disappear through the portal.

The Grimms stepped into the Editor's study. Granny took her own journal from her handbag and jotted a note: *The doors between stories are best traveled with empty stomachs.*

The Editor sat in his leather chair with a reviser resting at his feet, licking its lips as if it had just finished the last bite of a bucket of fried chicken. When he noticed the family, the old man leaped from his chair in shock.

"How did you get in here?"

"May I presume you are the Editor? Allow me to introduce myself," Granny said, ignoring his question. "My name is Relda Grimm. I believe you know my grandchildren, Sabrina and Daphne, as well as Puck. This is my son, Henry, and my daughter-in-law, Veronica. We are descendants of Trixie Grimm."

The Editor flashed her a dark look. "A most troublesome

woman, even if she did have a hand in my creation. She's responsible for many of my personal headaches."

"Well, I'm afraid I'm about to add to them," Granny replied. "We are in need of your services."

"You come to me for help?" the Editor asked, shocked. "You realize your granddaughters and the fairy betrayed me? After making a deal, they raised an army of characters who attacked me in my own sanctuary. They attempted to aid these revolutionaries in their quest to escape the Book."

"Sabrina!" Henry scolded.

"That's not exactly what happened," Sabrina said sheepishly.

"We didn't know they would attack him, Dad," Daphne added. "Besides, only two of them even made it all the way into the library."

"I doubt my daughters would knowingly betray you, or anyone," Veronica said to the man.

"Perhaps we can start over," Granny offered. "I can assure you, we will not be helping anyone escape the Book. In fact, we're here to remove two individuals who have no business in its pages."

"Mirror and the boy," the Editor said.

"Then you already know. Good. They've gone into 'Snow White and the Seven Dwarfs.' We would like to follow them, but there are barriers preventing it. If you would be so kind as to lower those barriers, we can catch Mirror and leave."

"There is no need. I have revisers pursuing them as we speak."

"You can't!" Daphne cried. "They might hurt our brother."

"It would be unfortunate," the Editor said. "But my responsibility is to these stories."

Henry grabbed the old man by the collar and pushed him hard against a bookshelf. Several volumes tumbled down on their heads. "That's my son in that story. If he gets hurt, I will revise you."

The Editor eyed him closely. "Your threats will not change my mind."

Henry pulled back a closed fist, but before he could strike the man, Granny spoke.

"Let him go, Henry. I think we can persuade him without violence."

Henry did as he was told. The Editor brushed off his suit and eyed the family. "Do you, now?"

"Yes, indeed," the old woman said, stepping over to the magic door. When she opened it, the wind carried the smell of wheat into the room. "If you think the children kept you busy, you have yet to see what I can do. Come along, family."

Henry and Veronica marched into the portal first.

"What are we going to do?" Daphne asked as she stepped across the threshold.

"Some good old-fashioned troublemaking," Granny Relda said

with a grin, and then turned to Puck. "Why don't we show the Editor here why they call you the Trickster King?"

Puck smiled and leaped into the void.

"What about me?" Pinocchio cried.

"Stay here," Granny said with a smile. "We'll be right back."

Sabrina slipped her hand into her grandmother's, stepped through the open doorway, and vanished.

9

THEY EMERGED ON A DUSTY ROAD LINED ON both sides by wheat so dry and white, Sabrina could almost hear it crying out for rain.

"Where are we, Mom?" Henry asked.

"Henry, I'm disappointed." The old woman smiled. "This is the setting for one of the most famous fairy tales ever told. And if I'm correct, all the action is just over that rise."

Puck ran ahead, and the family followed. When they reached the top of the crest, they looked down into a small valley. There, they spotted three tiny structures nestled along the road: one made from hay, the second from twigs, and the last from brick.

Daphne bit her palm and squeaked, but her happiness was short-lived. A hulking, hairy creature lumbered up to the house made of hay. It was the Big Bad Wolf.

He held a kazoo in his clawed hand. When he blew into it, a magical wind as powerful as a tornado blasted the little straw house. It exploded, leaving nothing behind but a pig with a familiar face. Ernest Hamstead was desperately clinging to a patch of grass with his little pig hooves. When he lost his grip, he went sailing across the valley until he was out of sight.

"That's not cool," Daphne said.

"I think it's hilarious." Puck giggled. "Really! I might wet myself if he does it again. Look, he's headed to the next house now."

"I never liked this story," Veronica admitted. "It's depressing."

"There goes the house of twigs," Puck said, howling with laughter.

Sabrina watched Mr. Swineheart disappearing into the distance.

"He's going to have some problems with the next house, Puck. Why don't you help him?" Granny Relda suggested.

"Really?" Puck asked, wiping away happy tears.

"Yes, go have some fun," the old woman said, and Puck ran off to join the Wolf.

"Relda!" Veronica cried.

"That's not nice," Daphne said.

"Remember, that's not the real Mr. Boarman," Granny said.

Sabrina watched Puck encourage the Big Bad Wolf to huff and puff again, but he was unable to cause the well-built brick structure any harm. So Puck spun on his heels and transformed into a woolly mammoth. He lowered his head and charged at the front door, knocking it off its hinges. The Wolf howled with glee, and then he raced into the house. A second later, Sabrina heard the Wolf's growls and the pig's squeals of fright.

"I did good, old lady?" Puck asked, having returned to his fairy form and traipsed back to the family's side.

Granny nodded and mussed the boy's hair. "You did very good, Puck."

Sabrina spotted revisers rushing down the street toward the brick house.

"I believe it's time to go," the old woman said matter-of-factly, just as a door materialized before them. Granny opened the door, and everyone stomped through.

Sabrina stared up at a tall ivory tower. In a window near the top was a beautiful princess with the longest red hair Sabrina had ever seen. It was braided as thick as a rope, and it hung down the side of the tower. Climbing it was a man Sabrina recognized as Prince Charming.

Granny pulled a pair of scissors from her handbag. She handed them to Puck, who giggled with delight. A moment later, he was airborne. He fluttered above the prince and started slicing the hair rope in two. When Puck had cut completely through it, Prince Charming fell to the ground and landed with one leg at a very unnatural angle.

Before long, the revisers descended, munching away at the story, and the family darted through another magic door.

They found themselves atop a grand staircase as a beautiful blond woman raced past. She hurried down the stairs, stumbled a bit, and lost her shoe. Once again, Prince Charming appeared, chasing her.

"It's Cinderella," Daphne whispered.

At the foot of the stairs, a pumpkin-shaped coach waited for Cinderella. But before she could climb inside, Granny told Puck to steal it. The boy flew down the stairs, leaped into the driver's seat, and shoved the driver to the ground. He grabbed the reins and sped off, leaving Cinderella stranded in front of Charming's castle. A moment later, a shimmering light engulfed the woman, and she transformed back into a filthy, overworked maid.

Prince Charming raced to her side with the glass slipper in his hands. "Excuse me, but are you the owner of—aw, geez, what is that smell?"

Cinderella ran off into the night, sobbing.

"Pretty girl, but not a big fan of soap, is she?" Prince Charming said to Henry.

A door appeared as Puck returned. His clothes were covered in slimy pumpkin. "That buggy changed while I was driving it," he complained. "I smell like a pie."

"You are doing very well," Granny commended him as revisers scurried up the staircase toward them. "Let's see what mess we can make next."

༄

"I don't think the children have showed up yet," Granny said to the family as they stood before a life-size gingerbread house with candy-cane windowpanes, a roof made of peanut brittle, and a walkway lined with gumdrops. They were clearly in Hansel and Gretel's story. "Puck, are you feeling hungry?"

The boy clapped his hands and rubbed them together greedily. "Starving!"

He descended upon on the house, chomping on parts of the roof and licking at the windows. He shoveled everything from the doorknob to the welcome mat into his mouth. In a matter of seconds, he was covered from head to toe in sticky, sugary candy. His hair was covered in cream filling, and icing ran down his shirt.

"Um, can I help with this one?" Daphne asked. Granny laughed. "Be my guest."

Daphne dove in with as much enthusiasm as Puck. She nibbled on the door and took a giant bite out of the house's chewy foundation.

As she and Puck ate, two kids appeared from out of the surrounding forest. They looked confused that other children were already eating the house. Puck waved them off. "Just go home, kids. We got this! A witch lives here, anyway. She's gonna put you in a cage and try to fatten you up. It's a really ugly story."

Hansel and Gretel shrugged and walked back the way they'd come.

"You're wrecking the stories on purpose," Sabrina said, somewhat embarrassed that it had taken her so long to understand her grandmother's plan.

"And I'm going to keep doing it until the Editor sees things my way," Granny Relda said.

"Here come the revisers," Sabrina said, nodding toward the edge of the woods.

"All right, time to move on," Granny said as a red door materialized. "Let's see if the Editor likes what we do to 'The Frog Prince.' I wonder if we can get the princess to try some frog legs for dinner."

The family stepped through the void, but they did not land where Granny Relda aimed. Instead, they found themselves back in the library. The Editor was staring at them in shock and exasperation.

"Enough. Enough! ENOUGH!!!! The chaos is overwhelming. I can't keep up. You have to stop this assault on the Book right now."

"There's a very simple way to get us to stop," Granny Relda said. "Let us into Snow White's story."

"Don't you understand?" The Editor scowled. "It's off-limits for a reason! It is unstable."

"I don't care," the old woman said. "I am Relda Grimm. I am the wife of Basil Grimm. The mother of Henry and Jacob Grimm, and the mother-in-law of Veronica Grimm. I'm the grandmother of Sabrina and Daphne Grimm, and the adopted grandmother to His Majesty, Puck. I am also the grandmother of the little boy Mirror has kidnapped. And I am an incredibly stubborn, willful, and unapologetic pain in the neck who gets what she wants. Now that we have been properly introduced, you should know one more thing about me—I don't care if every story in the Book falls apart and unravels reality itself. My family will always come first."

"Mirror is already in the story," Sabrina added. "You're going to have to revise anyway. What difference does it make if we go there, too?"

"All the difference in the world," the Editor said, and then his voice dropped to a murmur. "He's in there."

"He who?" Henry asked.

"I told your daughters about the great calamity that struck the Book. A member of the Everafter community manipulated the magic that fuels it. She changed the story of 'Snow White and the Seven Dwarfs' and bent it into something new, and drastic measures had to be taken in response. We deleted a character, erased him from existence—or at least from these pages. But we couldn't completely revise him. Hints of him remain, haunting the margins of all the stories like a shadow. His presence is most

felt between the lines of 'Snow White and the Seven Dwarfs.'
He pounds on the tale, demanding his freedom and promising
revenge. I cannot risk letting anyone into that story, because if
anything is altered, it could free him. And, trust me—you do
not want Atticus to walk the earth again."

"Who is Atticus?" Sabrina asked.

"It's best that I not tell you any more," the Editor said.

"I'm sorry, but we have to take the risk," Veronica said. "My
child is in that story, and we won't stop until he's safe. You can
help us, and maybe keep this Atticus under control, or we can do
it without you. But, either way, it's happening."

The Editor's resolve collapsed, like a boxer who suddenly gives
up in the middle of a fight. He shook his head in defeat, then
looked up to where his revisers clung to bookshelves.

"Might I have your attention?" he called out to them. A moment later, hundreds, if not thousands, of fat, hungry monsters
climbed down. They gathered at his feet, turning their blank faces
up to him.

"Someone has invaded Snow White's tale," he announced,
which caused the little creatures to erupt in nervous chatter. "His
name is Mirror. And he may cause a great deal of problems if we
do not stop him. I want him removed, and you are to do whatever
needs to be done to make that happen. This is a departure from
our usual rules. Mirror is a part of the story, and thus entitled to

makes changes, but—as you know—that story is dangerous. Any changes must be prevented. Mirror is also traveling with a small boy. The boy's safety is imperative."

The creatures twittered excitedly, and a chill shot up Sabrina's back.

"No, the child must be spared," the Editor demanded. "You are not to revise him. We are attempting to rescue him."

There was more chatter from the revisers, and the Editor frowned. He turned back to the family.

"They understand, but whether or not they will obey me is another story. They have their roles, as I have mine. The best I can do is give you a head start."

"What about me?" Pinocchio called. The boy sat on a stool in a corner listening to the plan. "You're not sending me back into those stories, are you?"

"I think you've caused enough trouble," the Editor said, and then turned to the Grimms. "The marionette will stay here with me."

"You hear that? I'm a marionette!" the boy yelled indignantly.

"Shut up!" the Grimms cried in unison.

The old man waved his hand, and a door materialized by the fireplace. He opened it and gestured into the emptiness beyond.

"Find him," the Editor begged. "Find Mirror and the boy. And then leave my book as quickly as you can."

ᑎᑌ

Sabrina looked around. She and her family stood in the middle of a crude cabin. A group of seven very short men were gathered around a beautiful woman as she swept the rough wooden floor.

"Well, who's hungry?" the woman asked, setting down her broom. She flashed a smile as bright as a spotlight. Her face was a collection of perfect features—bright red lips, skin like cream, hair as black as night, and bright blue eyes that sparkled like jewels.

"Ms. White!" Sabrina said.

Snow White looked confused. "Have we met?"

"Remember, *liebling*, she's not our Ms. White," Granny Relda said. "She's just walking history."

"Snow, you can't let anyone into this house," one of the little men said. Sabrina turned and recognized the speaker as the copy of another good friend, Mr. Seven.

"Your stepmother is trying to kill you," another dwarf added.

"I know, I know," Snow said, brushing them off as if it were nothing to worry about.

"She's already disguised herself as a peddler and choked you with a strand of lace," a bearded dwarf complained.

"Then you stuck that poisoned comb in your hair. Luckily, we came home from the mine before it killed you," a bald dwarf added.

"You need to be on your guard. You can't let anyone in when we are not with you," Mr. Seven said.

Snow White smiled wistfully as if she were thinking of something else entirely, then went back to sweeping the floor. "I'll do my best. I guess I'm just so gullible."

"Well, we better get back to work," Mr. Seven said. "Keep the doors locked."

"Will do!" Snow sang, but it was clear she wasn't listening.

The dwarfs shuffled out of the house, leaving the family alone with Snow. She turned to face them, confused.

"Still here?"

"You haven't noticed a magic mirror running around here with a little boy, have you?" Henry asked.

Snow leaned her broom against the wall. Her expression shifted from ditzy to deadly serious. "Have you come to change history again? This tale has been revised already. The Editor worked on it himself. Is he unhappy with how it's going?"

Suddenly, there was a rap at the door.

"That's the Wicked Queen," Snow said. "You should hide. We shouldn't alter anything further. It was almost impossible getting this story to make sense after all the changes."

The Grimms argued, but eventually Snow convinced them to hide under beds and listen as the story unfolded. Once everyone was out of sight, Snow went to an open window.

"I am not allowed to let anyone in," she called. "The dwarfs have forbidden me to do so."

An old woman's voice croaked from the other side of the window. "That is all right with me. I'll easily get rid of my apples. Here, I'll give you one of them."

"Don't do it," Daphne whispered.

"Hush!" Sabrina ordered.

"No, I can't accept anything," Snow replied.

"Are you afraid of poison? Look, I'll cut the apple in two. You can eat the red half, and I shall eat the white half."

Sabrina heard someone take a bite from the apple. A moment later, Snow White collapsed onto the floor. The old woman came into the cabin and stood over her.

"White as snow, red as blood, black as ebony wood. This time the dwarfs cannot awaken you," she recited.

When the old woman was gone, the family climbed out from under the beds and rushed over to Snow White.

"The people in these stories are morons," Sabrina said. "She knew the witch was coming to poison her, but she went through with the whole thing anyway."

Puck shook Snow. "Wakey-wakey, sleepyhead."

"She's enchanted," Sabrina explained. "She won't wake up until someone who truly loves her kisses her."

"So this is a horror story." Puck shuddered.

"The prince will be along to wake her soon," Granny said. "We can't waste any more time here. We need to find Mirror."

In the silence after Granny finished speaking, Sabrina heard the unmistakable sound of someone taking another crunchy bite of the apple. She turned to find Puck with a mouthful of fruit.

"Can't we stop and get something to eat? This puberty thing is making me all kinds of hungry. Oh!" He looked down at the apple in sudden realization and then fell to the floor in a heap.

"Puck, no!" Henry cried.

"I can't believe you! Where is your brain?" Sabrina shouted at the unconscious boy.

"In his defense, I don't think he knows this story very well," Daphne said. "His parents probably didn't read him too many fairy tales when he was little . . . four thousand years ago."

"Aaargh!" Sabrina growled. "We have to find Mirror and stop him—not carry Sleepy Steven around. What should we do?"

"We can leave Puck in one of these beds," Henry suggested. "He'll be safe here. When it's all said and done, we'll come back and get him."

"What about the revisers?" Sabrina asked as her father hauled Puck's limp body to the nearest cot. "What if they come before we get back?"

"We'll watch him," a voice said. The dwarfs had returned.

Mr. Seven was in the lead. "The Editor explained everything. Follow the path to the castle. That's where you'll find Mirror."

"C'mon, *lieblings*," Granny Relda said as she pushed the cottage door open.

The family raced up a road, hurrying deeper and deeper into the woods. Sabrina worried that they would never make it to the castle, that Atticus might attack at any moment. Luckily, she was wrong.

"There it is," Daphne said, pointing up the road. An enormous castle built from black stones sat high on a hill. Its two towers reached toward the clouds. Each bore an ebony flag twisting in the wind.

"Great," Sabrina grumbled. "Nothing like a spooky castle for an ultimate showdown."

With their legs aching and their lungs tight, the Grimms raced across the drawbridge. The waters below were filled with horrible leathery crocodiles and odd spiked beasts. They snapped and growled as the family raced overhead.

In the castle itself, they found a huge room filled with paintings of an elegant woman. She had dark hair and was dressed in bloodred robes. In one, her hand rested on the head of a cheetah. Sabrina recognized the woman at once; she was Bunny Lancaster—also known as the Wicked Queen. There was no sign of Mirror or the little boy.

"Look! Stairs!" Veronica called, pointing behind a tapestry.

Sabrina helped her grandmother scale the steep staircase.

Huffing and puffing when they reached the top, they hurried down a long, empty hallway, only to face another flight of stairs.

"Can't anyone do their evil stuff on the first floor?" Henry complained.

"Or at least put in an elevator," Daphne said.

They climbed the second flight and were stopped in their tracks by a heavy wooden door. Through it, they heard a terrified scream followed by a crash of breaking glass.

"Stay close," Henry whispered to his family. He pushed open the door and revealed a horrible scene. Mirror held the Wicked Queen off the floor, one hand wrapped around her throat. Her face was blue, and her feet were kicking wildly.

"I was hoping you wouldn't have to see this, Relda. My mother and I have a complicated relationship," Mirror said, keeping his attention on the witch. "You look surprised, Mommy. Of all the people in the world, you should know why I'm so angry. You imprisoned me, then gave me away. What kind of mother are you?!"

His rage echoed off the walls. In the far corner, a small child let out a whimpering cry. It was Sabrina and Daphne's baby brother!

Henry raced to him, but a blast of lightning from Mirror's free hand stopped him in his tracks.

"Not so fast, Hank," Mirror said. He tossed the witch across the room.

"I am not your mother," the Wicked Queen choked. "If it's

revenge you're after, you should have stayed in the real world. You must stop. What you're doing here in the Book could have terrible consequences."

Mirror's eyes glowed bright, and the air crackled. He stuck out an angry finger at the woman. "As always, you deny me."

A mirror hung on the wall. It was identical to the one they had in Granny Relda's home. Suddenly, its glass swirled and a bulbous, intimidating face appeared. It was Mirror—or, rather, the Book of Everafter version. His expression was panicked.

"There is no need for this violence," the fake magic mirror said.

"So, this is what I look like on the other side? I'm really quite fearsome," Mirror said, approaching the reflection.

"What do you want?" the Wicked Queen asked, finally getting to her feet.

After a long moment, Mirror stalked back to the Wicked Queen. "I want you to use your considerable magical talents to make me real. I want—"

Suddenly, there was a tremendous lurching sensation. Everything shook—the ground, the air, even the colors of objects scattered around the room. Sabrina felt like she was trapped in a snow globe held by an overexcited child.

"What was that?" Granny Relda said.

"This story is unstable," the Wicked Queen said. "It can't take any more changes."

"Then we better get crackin'," Mirror said, grabbing the witch roughly by the arm and dragging her across the room to a table covered by a tarp.

The Wicked Queen looked around as if hoping for an escape, but then her shoulders slumped in surrender. She pulled the tarp off to reveal a dozen empty frames large enough for mirrors and several jars filled with blobs of black liquid. The substance in each jar squirmed as if it were alive.

"You don't understand, Mirror. I can't just make you into a person. You are an enchantment, a spell—nothing more than a few rare ingredients and an ancient incantation. Here, I'll show you." She opened one of the jars and poured the black glob into her hand. It slithered up her arm like a snake, but she wrangled it back into her palm. She spoke a few unintelligible words, and her hand turned a bright, hot red.

She dropped the goo into one of the frames, and it spread over the empty space, shining brighter and brighter, like a television screen. Then she placed her hand over it, muttered a few more ancient words, and removed her hand. The black turned to silver, and a scarlet handprint burned at its center. It reminded Sabrina of the mark Mirror used, the Scarlet Hand.

Mirror smiled. "That image was the first thing I saw when I was born. It's quite a unique symbol—intimidating, powerful. Don't you agree, Relda? You must have seen it all over Ferryport Landing."

Granny shook her head in disgust.

The red print faded, and a face appeared in the frame. It was a burly man with short gray hair, a full beard, and a heavy sweater.

"Awaiting your instructions," it said in a gruff tone.

"A fascinating demonstration," Mirror said, then gestured to the jars. "If you can put that energy into a frame, then you can take it out, correct?"

The Wicked Queen's eyes grew wide. "I suppose I could, but I would have to place it in something else—a new vessel—or the magic would die."

"Allow me to introduce my vessel," Mirror said. He snatched Sabrina's brother off the floor. "I want you to put me into him."

"You want to take over his body?" the Book of Everafter version of Mirror cried.

"Living inside a human being will give me my freedom, not only from the Hall of Wonders, but from the town of Ferryport Landing. I will be both Everafter and human. I will be able to pass through the barrier that traps the rest of the fools."

"The boy's soul will not be strong enough to survive," the Wicked Queen said.

"Can you do it?" Mirror demanded, ignoring her concern.

The Wicked Queen nodded. "Yes, but—"

"No!" Veronica cried, rushing forward. "If you want a body, you can take mine!"

Mirror shot a blast of lightning at her feet, and she fell backward.

"No offense, Veronica, but I'd like to live a long, full life. I want the boy."

"None of this had to happen, Mirror. You could have come to me," Granny Relda said. "I would have done everything in my power to set you free."

"Relda, I have no doubt you would have tried. You and your family have been very kind to me, but no amount of kindness is equal to freedom. Inevitably, you would have failed to find a solution. Because you are human, you would eventually die, and I would be passed on to a new owner. And who knows who those new owners would have been? I could have landed back in the hands of tyrants. I am more than property, and my freedom cannot wait another day." He turned back to the Wicked Queen. "All right, Mother. It's time you finally gave me a birthday present."

"Don't do it!" Daphne exclaimed.

The Wicked Queen shook her head sadly at the little girl. "I have to put my faith in the Editor. He will have to fix these changes. I just hope the story survives the process." She stepped toward Mirror, her hand glowing red. "You may want to set the boy on the ground."

Mirror did as he was told, and the witch placed her hand on Mirror's head. He screamed in agony as her hand burned his skin.

Then, a black glob like the ones in the jars seeped out of his mouth and hovered before Mirror's blank eyes. When the Queen let go of him, Mirror's body collapsed to the ground and liquefied into a silver, reflective fluid.

"Bunny, you don't have to finish this," Granny said.

"If I don't, he'll take someone else in this room. Maybe even me. You don't want him to have my power."

She stood the boy up and waved her red hand just over his face, and the ebony liquid shot into his mouth. If he was hurt or distressed, he showed no sign. The only change was the expression on his face. His youthful smile and sparkling eyes were replaced with a hardened, ageless intelligence. He looked down at the silver puddle and studied his face in the reflection.

"Fascinating," he said.

"No!" Veronica cried, bursting into tears. Henry's head fell in despair.

The toddler turned to the Grimms. He lifted his little hands, and his fingertips crackled with magical power. "Very good. My powers work, as well."

"The Editor will stop this," Sabrina said. "He'll revise all of this."

"Oh, I'm afraid he's going to have his hands full with other problems," the boy said. "You see, I'm going to bring this whole story tumbling down."

"How?" Sabrina asked.

"I'm going to kill its main character," the child replied, his eyes glowing with power. His little body hovered off the ground and zipped through the castle window into the open sky. Sabrina and Daphne rushed forward and watched him soaring down the mountain and toward the Seven Dwarfs' cottage.

A door materialized, and the Editor appeared, looking panicked. "I had hoped to avoid all of this, but it appears I cannot. What Mirror's about to do may have consequences in the real world. We all have to stop him at any cost!"

10

THE WICKED QUEEN LED EVERYONE DOWN THE many flights of stairs, out of the castle, and to a stable where several horses waited. Henry and Veronica helped the girls and Granny Relda onto their mounts, then took two for themselves. The Wicked Queen climbed onto a frightening black stallion with angry eyes. Seconds later, they were all bolting back down the road to the cabin.

"Revisers!" Daphne screamed. Hundreds of creatures were eating away at the trees and shrubs lining their path.

"Pray they work quickly," the witch said.

"Pray? Those things are monsters," Sabrina said.

"Those things may be the only way of keeping the story intact. They must devour it before it falls apart. If not, something far worse than a reviser may be let loose."

"Are you talking about Atticus? What's so bad about him?" Sabrina asked.

"He was responsible for unspeakable horrors and tragedies. It's best if we don't even mention his name."

Back at the cottage, they found two glass coffins resting on a platform in the garden. In one rested the lovely Snow White. In the other was Puck. It seemed impossible that they were sleeping, as a terrible fight raged inside the house. Through the window, she could see all of the Seven Dwarfs battling with Mirror, still embodying the very young boy. He zipped around in the air like a mosquito, firing bolts of lightning.

Mr. Seven broke from the fight and rushed outside to meet the group.

"He has no idea of the damage he's doing," Seven said. "And he won't listen to reason."

"We spotted revisers over the hill," the Wicked Queen said. "Perhaps they'll save us this time."

A man on a great gray horse galloped out of the woods. He was handsome, with dark brown hair and blue eyes.

"Billy Charming," Daphne gasped.

"The Editor told me to get the real people out of the Book before the story is broken. My brother may soon be free," Prince Charming announced.

A red door appeared behind him.

"Your brother?" Granny Relda said. "You don't have a brother."

"You and your family must leave at once," the Wicked Queen said, opening the door.

"We won't go without my son," Henry said. "Can you remove Mirror from his body?"

"Yes—but like I said, he'll just jump into someone else."

"Do it!" Granny demanded.

The Wicked Queen's hand turned red once more. She reached toward the little boy, and his body flew to her as if drawn by a magnet. The witch's burning hand clamped down on his head, and Mirror's voice cried out in agony.

"No!" he screamed.

The little boy fainted, and Veronica swept him into her arms. All the while, the witch drew Mirror's black life force from the small, frail child. Soon, the connection was broken, but the witch could not control it. The black blob darted around the group, desperate to find a new vessel. Sabrina watched, both horrified and fascinated, until it raced to her face and tried to force its way into her mouth. She ground her teeth together to keep it out. Frustrated, it darted toward her sister.

"Don't open your mouth!" Sabrina shouted. Daphne was doing all she could to resist, but Mirror was incredibly strong.

It was then that Sabrina overcame the doubt that had plagued her for so many days. Sure, she'd made mistakes, but when it was a matter of life and death involving a loved one, she always knew what to do. She raced to Daphne's side, prepared to sacrifice herself. She would take Mirror into her body and hope that her family could find a way to stop him.

"Take me!" The words rang through the air, but they didn't come from Sabrina. Granny Relda was hovering over Daphne, inviting Mirror to use her.

"Mom! No!" Henry shouted.

The old woman turned to her family and gave them all a weak smile. "Daphne isn't strong enough, Henry. If Mirror uses me, he can only cause so much trouble for so long. I'm old, with creaky joints and arthritis. If he's going to take over the world, then the world should only have to suffer a little while."

"Granny! Please!" Sabrina begged.

"I love you, *liebling*," Granny said, blowing her kisses. "Take care of Puck—he's one of mine, too."

She turned and grabbed the black blob suffocating Daphne. It resisted, but she held tight. Eventually, it surrendered and zipped into the old woman's mouth. Granny's face went pale, losing its rosy color. Her bright green eyes flashed white hot, and her sweet, soft smile was replaced with an angry, bitter scowl.

"You have ruined everything!" Mirror's voice erupted out of the old woman. "Look at this body!"

"Vile creature," Prince Charming said. He pulled his sword and waved it threateningly at Granny Relda. "Release your hold on that woman."

Sparks crackled from the old woman's fingertips. "You ridiculous oaf. Do you think I would stay in this body if I had a choice?"

Energy blasted from Granny Relda's hands and shocked the Prince. While he was distracted, Mirror snatched Charming's sword away from him and thrust it into the prince's gut. He fell over and moved no more.

The world shook so violently that Sabrina was knocked to the ground. Before she could stand, there was a second explosion. This one was louder, and the blast of wind that accompanied it was so hot, it scorched her face, neck, and hands. But the third explosion was the one that frightened her. Fissures formed in the earth, allowing steam to escape from deep below. It wasn't a mist or a fog—it was alive, made up of something old and angry.

"He's killed a main character," the Wicked Queen cried. "He's broken the story."

"Atticus is free!" Mr. Seven shouted.

"Everyone must go," the Wicked Queen ordered. "Before it's too late!"

There was a fourth and final explosion, and from the smoke and mist a wild, red-haired brute of a man appeared. He wore a black tunic and heavy boots, and he had scars up and down his hairy arms. He held a long staff, a heavy steel ball hanging by a chain from its end. The man studied Sabrina. He smiled, but it was not friendly, more like the grin of a lucky tiger who has just stumbled upon wounded prey. His attention shifted to Prince Charming's lifeless body, and he laughed.

"Brother, I'm disappointed," Atticus said, and then kicked the man in the ribs. "I wanted to kill you myself."

While everyone watched the hulking man, Granny Relda rushed to the red door. Sabrina watched her turn for a moment to look back at the family. Her eyes locked on Sabrina's, and she frowned, then sneered. A moment later, she darted through the doorway and disappeared.

"She's getting away!" Henry cried.

"What is this?" Atticus demanded, leaping into their path. "Is this a doorway to the real world? It is, isn't it?"

He looked down at his dead brother and let out a howling laugh.

"Perhaps I will get to kill you after all, brother!" he continued, and then he leaped through the door and vanished.

"Kids, we have to go!" Henry shouted over the earthquake that was shaking everything apart. He opened one of the glass caskets and scooped Puck off his cushion.

"No arguments there," Daphne cried, then pointed down the road. Thousands of pink revisers were scuttling in their direction, devouring everything they came across.

Veronica clung to her son and dashed through the doorway. Henry followed with Puck flung over his shoulder. Sabrina and Daphne rushed through the portal as the world around them was erased into nothing.

ᕲᕝ

They found themselves back in the Hall of Wonders, in the room that held the Book of Everafter. Pinocchio followed soon after, flying out of the book and landing unceremoniously on his rump.

"The Editor threw me out," he grumbled as he rubbed his sore bottom. "He said we have to stop Atticus. He's apparently as dangerous in this world as he was in the Book."

"Atticus is going to have to wait until we find my mother," Henry said.

The family exited and then locked the room. They started the long trek out of the Hall of Wonders, wondering if they would find Atticus or Granny Relda along the way, but they didn't. It was almost as if both had vanished into thin air. Sabrina wondered if they had escaped the Book at all.

Eventually, they came to the portal leading to Granny's home. When they stepped through, they came out in Granny's front yard. Sabrina turned to look at what was left of their home. Very little was still standing. Pinocchio's marionettes had let a lot of dangerous creatures out of the Hall of Wonders. Monsters had stampeded through the mirror and demolished what generations of Grimms had called their own. Luckily, the family's Great Dane, Elvis, was unharmed. He raced forward and knocked Daphne onto the grass, showering her with happy licks. She kissed him back, then stood to introduce him to the newest member of the family. Veronica leaned forward so the big dog could sniff the little boy. Elvis covered the child's face with one huge slurpy kiss, and the boy giggled.

Henry eased Puck to the ground and leaned against the family's ancient car, another miraculous survivor of the chaos that had torn apart their home. He scratched his head, looked around at the mess, and frowned.

"I have to go back in to get the journals," he said, referring to the leather-bound books every member of the family used to document their time in Ferryport Landing. "We'll need them. There could be something in them that might help us defeat Mirror and deal with that Atticus person."

Veronica begged him to reconsider, but Henry said he didn't have a choice. The journals were the family's most important possessions. Everyone held their breath when he entered the ruins and didn't let it out again until he came back with two heavy sacks filled with books. He set them in the trunk of the car, then tied the magic mirror to the top. The Hall of Wonders was still inside it and might prove useful.

"Well?" Daphne said to Sabrina.

"Well, what?" she asked.

"You have to kiss Puck."

Sabrina wasn't sure she'd heard her sister correctly. "What?"

"You have to kiss him. Someone who loves him needs to kiss him to break the sleeping spell."

"Absolutely not!" Henry shouted.

"It has to be a romantic kiss, too," Daphne added slyly.

"Well, then he's going to be asleep forever, because there isn't a single romantic thing about him," Sabrina said.

The entire family gave her knowing looks until her face turned red with embarrassment.

"I don't love him! Really! It won't work," she insisted.

"Who are you trying to fool? I barely know you, but even I understand the two of you are an item," Pinocchio said.

"Children, please, let's not talk about this anymore," Veronica said. "Your father is about to have a heart attack, and to be honest, I don't think I'm ready for Sabrina to have a boyfriend, either."

"He's not my boyfriend!" Sabrina cried, then turned her attention to the sleeping boy. Puck was smelly, rude, mean, selfish, stupid, and immature. He wasn't the kind of boy girls fell in love with. He was the kind they stayed fifty yards from at all times. She didn't love him. She knew she didn't. Did she? Still, the whole family was staring at her. If she didn't at least try, they'd just keep nagging. What else could she do? Fine! She'd kiss him, but then she'd brush, floss, and gargle the first chance she got.

Daphne rolled her eyes. "Geez, enough with the buildup. Just do it."

"This isn't going to help," she said, then leaned in and pressed her lips to his. A tiny charge startled her, and she stepped back. It hadn't hurt. In fact, it was nice and . . . surprising. "See! I told you I didn't love him. That was a complete waste of time."

Puck's eyes flickered open. He sat up, rubbed his eyes, and grinned. "So, what did I miss?"

"I'm going to go somewhere far away and pretend I didn't see that," Henry said. He and Veronica took their son and drifted into the backyard. Daphne grabbed Pinocchio by the collar and dragged him along, too.

"Geez, puppet boy," she said. "Can't you take a hint? They need a little time alone."

"I was a marionette!" he shouted. "Why is that so hard to under-stand?"

"Why is everyone being so weird?" Puck asked.

"Mirror is inside Granny," Sabrina explained.

"How did I miss that?"

"You were under a sleeping spell."

"Really? How did you wake me up?"

Once again, Sabrina felt herself flush.

"You didn't," Puck said as his own face turned pink.

Sabrina nodded. "I did."

"Then that means . . ." He trailed off.

Sabrina sat down next to Puck in the grass. They were quiet for a long time, looking at everything but each other.

Finally, Puck broke the silence. "Let's not change."

"Huh?"

"The insults. The pranks. Let's not change."

"I don't know what you're talking about."

"Someday you and I are getting married." Puck sighed, as if terribly depressed. "The cruel hand of fate won't let us escape it. Worse, my own body is betraying me. I'm getting older every day. So, if we have to get married and have a million babies, I hope our relationship will be built on mutual disgust and an endless barrage of ridicule. It feels like the only thing I can count on right now. I don't want something dumb like respect and affection ruining what we have."

Sabrina laughed. "OK, on the extreme outside chance that you and I get married, I promise to insult you every day. But, you know, there's a much bigger chance you won't have to spend the rest of your life with me."

"You said you went to the future and we were married," Puck said. "We can't escape destiny."

"We didn't see *the* future. We saw *a* future," Sabrina said. "When we got back to the present, Daphne, Charming, and I started changing everything we could to prevent it from happening. We haven't changed a lot, but we have changed some things. Snow White was dead in the future, but we managed to save her life. Daphne's face was horribly scarred, and we prevented that, too. We can't know for sure, but the changes might have altered everything."

Puck sat back, deep in thought. "So, you and I might not have to do all that mushy stuff and have kids and buy a house and get a mortgage? I might not have to get a job or take baths or start reading?"

Sabrina shrugged. "If we rescue Granny Relda and stop Mirror for good, we will change a lot. It's impossible to tell until we get older."

"Awesome! Let's kick Mirror's butt," he said.

Sabrina smiled, but down deep Puck's comment hurt. Not that she wanted her whole life planned out for her in advance. She was only twelve years old. She wanted some mystery, and a feeling of being able to choose her own path. Still, Puck . . . he was special. He was her first kiss. Her first crush. Her first everything. Why couldn't he just say she was special to him, too?

"Thank you, Sabrina Grimm."

"For what?"

"Don't torture me! I won't say it out loud. Just . . . you know, in four thousand years no one has felt . . . I really . . . you're . . . Oh, just forget it!" he said. He took a deep breath. "Geez, Grimm. You're rank."

It was the closest thing she was going to get to an "I love you, too," she realized.

Daphne and their parents returned with the baby.

"Baby X is so cute," Daphne said. "I'm going to eat him."

"You know, we can't call him Baby X," Henry said.

"We've come up with a name," Veronica said.

"Please tell me it isn't Oohg," Sabrina replied.

"No. We're going to name him after your grandfather Basil." Henry beamed.

"Basil Grimm," Daphne said, rolling the name over her tongue. "Works for me!"

"So, what's next?" Puck asked. "The old lady has turned into a madman, which means no more free meals for me. We have to get her back."

Henry sighed. "I'm not sure what to do first."

Sabrina looked around at her family. Once again, they needed a leader, but this time Sabrina wasn't so worried about stepping forward to do the job.

"Mirror has some horrible plans, and Atticus sounds like he's going to be a big problem," Sabrina said. "We need to gather the others. Puck, you find Uncle Jake, Mr. Canis, Charming, and Snow White. Take Pinocchio with you. Mom, Dad, Daphne—we need to go see the real Wicked Queen, and unfortunately, we're going to have to get some help from someone I'd rather not see again."

"Baba Yaga," Daphne groaned.

Sabrina nodded. "We're going to need this town's most power-ful people, because if we can't stop Mirror, it may very well be the end of the world."

ENJOY THIS
SNEAK PEEK FROM

THE SISTERS GRIMM

~ THE COUNCIL OF MIRRORS ~

1

OCTOBER 14

My name is Sabrina Grimm, and this is my journal. My family has been bugging me to write in it for a while. I tried a few times before, but I never really wanted to get all that involved with the family business. I wanted to be a normal girl, living in New York City. I wanted to go to school and have friends and buy bagel sandwiches at the deli on York and 88th Street every morning.

If you're reading this, it means you know that didn't happen. It also means you're either Puck (stop snooping, stinkface!) or you're a future Grimm. Maybe you're like me, and you didn't choose this life. Instead, you got dumped into it, and nothing makes sense. Well, I suppose the least I can do is try to help you. There's a lot of stuff you need to know, so you might want to sit down for this.

You know those bedtime stories your parents read to you at night? The ones filled with fairies, giants, witches, monsters, mad tea parties, sleeping princesses, and cowardly lions? They're not stories. They're history. They're based on actual events and actual people. These real-life fairy-tale characters call themselves Everafters, and a lot of them are still alive today.

That's where our family comes in. We're Grimms, descendants of one half of the Brothers Grimm, and for hundreds of years we've kept an eye on the Everafter community. Believe me, it's no picnic.

OK, I know you're probably thinking I've been sitting too close to the microwave, but I'm telling the truth. I didn't believe any of this at first, either, so let me start at the beginning. Two years ago, my parents, Henry and Veronica Grimm, mysteriously disappeared. My sister, Daphne, and I thought they had abandoned us, but it turned out Mom and Dad had been kidnapped (long story). Enter Granny Relda, our long-lost grandmother who we thought was dead (an even longer story). She brought us to live with her in a little town called Ferryport Landing, where most of the Everafters live.

You've probably never heard of Ferryport Landing. As I write this, there's an angry mob of ogres, trolls, talking animals, and other assorted monsters running loose on its streets, terrorizing everyone. Anyone with any sense at all has left or gone into hiding—but not us! Oh, no, not the Grimms! Our family has no interest in running for safety, so we're knee-deep in trouble, and things don't look like they're going to get any better.

But you still need to know about Ferryport Landing and every-

thing that happened here. Of course, there might not be any more Grimms after me. I might be dead, and then there won't be anyone to read this journal. Like I said, things are looking pretty bleak. But that's enough backstory for today. I'll write more when I can. For now, I have to go save the world.

Sabrina snapped her journal shut and tucked it into the folds of her sleeping bag for safekeeping. She rubbed her eyes and stretched, sore from sleeping on the cold marble floor of her new bedroom.

Not that the place where she and Daphne were sleeping could actually be called a bedroom. A bedroom contained—at the very least—a bed and a window and a place to put your clothes. The girls were sleeping in an empty room with stone walls and more than a few cobwebs draped in the corners. Every night, Sabrina told herself that this was temporary, that someday they would have a real room again. But to make that happen, she knew she had to get to work.

Sabrina dug into the foot of her sleeping bag for the drumstick and rusty cowbell she kept there, then padded over to her still-sleeping sister. She called out to Daphne, even gave her a few shakes, but the little girl could sleep through a tornado. Waking her often required drastic measures.

DONK! Sabrina felt the sound of the cowbell deep in the pit of her stomach, but Daphne did not stir.

"Time to wake up!" *DONK! DONK! DONK!*

"You are a terrible human being," Daphne croaked, pulling her sleeping bag over her head. As she sank inside, a big snout popped out. It belonged to Elvis, the family's Great Dane. He eyed Sabrina sourly.

"C'mon. Get up, both of you. We've got stuff to do," Sabrina said.

Daphne grumbled but did as she was told. She and the dog crawled out of the sleeping bag, got to their feet, and yawned at the same time. Daphne scratched her armpit, and Elvis went to work on his rump.

Sabrina noticed a book hiding in the folds of her sister's bedding, and she frowned. The Book of Everafter was a collection of fairy tales, but it was also a magical object. Its readers could step into its stories, alter them, and in turn change things back in the real world. It should have been behind locked doors, but Daphne was determined to keep a close eye on it.

"You shouldn't leave that lying around," Sabrina said. "Hasn't it caused enough trouble? What if it falls into the wrong hands?"

Daphne snatched it up. "Elvis is protecting it."

"At least tell me you've found something in there that will help us free Granny from Mirror."

The little girl shook her head. "There are a lot of stories—like, thousands! I'm still reading."

"We're running out of time, Daphne," Sabrina scolded.

"I know!" her sister shouted.

The girls were silent for a moment, and the tension melted away.

"I'm sorry," Sabrina said. "I know you're doing your best. Let's see if anyone else is having any luck."

She led Daphne and Elvis out of their room and into a vast hallway with a barrel ceiling as high as the sky. Hundreds—maybe even thousands—of doors lined both walls. The rooms they hid had once housed monsters and magical items but had recently been looted. Now most of the rooms sat empty, but others still held a few surprises.

The sisters walked along the hall until they reached the door they were looking for. They pushed it open and stepped inside. Mirrors—twenty-five of them—were mounted on the walls.

Sabrina and her family had moved the magic mirrors to one of the Hall of Wonders' newly empty rooms that was closer to the portal, so that they could more easily access the Room of Reflections, as they called it. But only five of the mirrors remained intact. The others were busted and broken. Sabrina and Daphne were collecting the shards one by one and carefully gluing them onto the walls. When light hit the fragments just right, they created a dazzling effect.

Instead of reflecting back Sabrina's image, the five intact mirrors each showed a bird's-eye view of Ferryport Landing. Ugly purple and black clouds hovered in the sky. The clouds had appeared two days prior, blasting the town with lightning and ear-smashing claps of thunder. "Hello, Mirrors," said Daphne.

The reflections suddenly glowed with an otherworldly light. The surfaces of the glass shimmered and rippled, and when they finally stilled, four odd faces materialized. In the first mirror, a brutal barbarian named Titan appeared; the second showed a seventies-era nightclub owner who went by the name Donovan; the third was a laid-back beach lover with long dreadlocks named Reggie; and the fourth was Fanny, a roller-skating waitress with fire-engine-red hair. The fifth mirror remained empty.

"Well, hello, darlings," Fanny said in her thick southern accent. She chewed gum while she talked and blew bubbles between phrases. "I think that one of the reasons we couldn't find your granny is because we were lookin' in the wrong places."

"Well, the world is pretty big," Sabrina said.

"That's just it, honey. She's not out in the world. She's still here in Ferryport Landing!" the waitress cried, then did a happy dance on her roller skates. She lived in the Diner of Wonders, an old-fashioned ice-cream shop, complete with red counters and matching stools. Behind her, a milkshake machine hummed, and a jukebox waited patiently for nickels.

"What?" Sabrina asked.

"But stealing a human body was Mirror's plan for getting out of the town. Why hasn't he gone?" Daphne asked.

"Well, I don't rightly know," Fanny admitted. "But I do have a theory."

"And that is?" Sabrina urged.

"He's stuck, Ms. Sabrina," Reggie said from his Island of Wonders. "The bad weather outside isn't a storm. It's his temper tantrum."

Daphne slipped her hand into Sabrina's and gave her a hopeful smile. Mirror had hijacked their grandmother's body two days ago in the hope of skipping town and taking over the world. With his powers, there would be little any human being could do to stop him. But now . . .

"Serves him right!" Titan roared from the Dungeon of Wonders. He was a rugged man with long, rust-colored hair and a scraggly beard. He often worked himself up into a blustery rage, turning his face the shade of his mane. Titan made Sabrina nervous. The medieval torture chamber he lived inside was filled with spikes, sharp weapons, and boiling oils. But he seemed to be on the Grimms' side. "If only I were a living, breathing man, I would put a painful end to our brother's atrocities!"

"He's no brother of mine," Reggie grumbled. "The firstborn is a scoundrel of the worst kind."

"Firstborn?" Sabrina asked.

"That's what we've been calling him, sister. He was the first magic mirror the Wicked Queen ever made—you know, the prototype," Donovan explained, as he fixed his Afro with a comb. He lived inside the Disco of Wonders, a nightclub that never closed with a dance floor that lit up like a rainbow.

"Anything is better than his other name," Fanny said. *The Master* is—"

"Creep-tastic?" Daphne asked, pretending to shudder.

Sabrina didn't have to pretend. Every time Mirror's name was mentioned, it felt like her blood flash froze in her veins. How could she have ever called him a friend? She had confessed all her hopes and fears to him. She had trusted him, but he was using her, all the while making his horrible plans. The second he got the chance, he betrayed her and her entire family.

"Whatever his name, our brother will pay! He has stained the honor of magic mirrors everywhere!" Titan roared, pounding on his chest.

"You mean, the four of us?" Donovan said. "We're all that's left, big daddy."

Titan snarled. "All the more reason to protect our legacy."

"Calm down, sugar. You'll get your blood pressure up again," Fanny said as she applied a coat of ruby-red lipstick. "Now that we know where the firstborn is, it's time to focus our energies on catching him and freeing Relda Grimm from his control."

"Please tell me you have some ideas," Sabrina said. Her plea was met with heartbreaking silence.

Daphne sighed. "Well, at least we know where Granny is now. How about Uncle Jake?"

Donovan shook his head. "He's been harder to find than your granny, dancing queen. He disappeared right off the map."

"We can sense his presence, but we can't pinpoint it," Reggie added. "Wherever he is, he doesn't want to be found, and I think he's using some serious mojo to make sure it stays that way."

"Well, I'm worried about him, but Uncle Jake has always been able to take care of himself," Sabrina said. "Right now, we should focus on finding Granny. Now that we know she's still in town, we can rescue—"

"Forget it! You and Daphne are sitting this one out," said a voice from behind her. Sabrina spun around to find her parents approaching. Her mother, Veronica, was carrying Basil, her two-year-old brother. Henry, her father, was dressed in a heavy jacket and hiking boots. He looked exhausted. "Mirror is way too dangerous," he argued.

"But danger is my middle name," Daphne said.

"Your middle name is Delilah, young lady," Veronica said. "Some jobs are for grown-ups. Besides, I could use your help with Basil."

"Babysitting?" Sabrina cried.

"Your mother was up all night with him," Henry said. "He's . . . he . . . well, he won't sleep, and he isn't eating."

As if to illustrate Henry's point, Basil cried and squirmed in his mother's arms, pounding on her chest with his little fists.

"Just tell them the truth, Henry," Veronica said. "Basil misses Mirror."

Sabrina scowled. Basil had been kidnapped as a newborn by Mirror, who planned to put his own mind inside the boy's human body. Basil barely knew his real family—he only knew his captor.

Veronica looked pained. It frightened Sabrina to see her strong, confident parents so fragile.

"So, what is your plan of action, Henry?" Titan asked. "I hope you aren't going to chase Mirror down and confront him."

"No." Henry shook his head. "For now, I think it's best if we keep our distance. But I do want to get a good look at him. Maybe I can spot a weakness. That thunderstorm he's conjuring has been hovering over the southern end of town for a day. I assume he's at the train station off of Route Nine. I'll start there."

"I'd feel better if someone was going with you," Veronica said.

"Someone is," Henry replied as he buttoned his jacket.

Sabrina heard a fluttering of wings and a voice above their heads. "Incoming!" Something wet and sticky landed on her head with a splat and trickled down her face. It smelled like the livestock tent at a state fair. Sabrina looked up and saw Puck floating above her, laughing and aiming another balloon filled with funky, sloshing green ooze right at her.

"What's in those balloons?" Sabrina growled as she wiped the muck off her face.

"I don't have a clue. I found it collecting in a pool near the sewage treatment plant. It was just sitting there—free for the taking! Can you imagine?" He flung the second balloon, and it hit her in the shoulder, splattering all over her neck. "This is grade-A filth! It's top of the line."

Sabrina clenched her fists and growled.

Puck looked genuinely shocked by her anger. "You're mad? You should be honored. There's a list of people a mile long I could throw this slop at, and you're at the top!"

"C'mon!" Henry shouted to the boy fairy, and Puck darted to join him, narrowly escaping the knuckle sandwich Sabrina was preparing to serve him.

"You're really leaving us here?" Daphne cried. "Again?"

"We are," Henry confirmed.

"You can't keep us locked up in this mirror forever! We could help you," Sabrina shouted, but Henry waved her off. He and Puck stormed out of the Room of Reflections, through the portal that led to the real world, and then they were gone.

"Mom! This is ridiculous. Granny Relda trained us for things like this. We've got crazy skills," Daphne grumbled.

Veronica patted them each on the shoulder. "Your dad's right, girls. It's too dangerous. And believe it or not, there really is plenty to do around here. Go find Pinocchio. He could start lending a hand. We are feeding him, after all."

When the girls were out of earshot of their mother, Sabrina turned to Daphne.

"Get your jacket," Sabrina said.

"Uh-oh! I know that look," Daphne said, grinning. "You're thinking about shenanigans!"

"Shenanigans?"

"It's my new word. It means 'fun troublemaking,'" Daphne explained. "You've got a plan to get into some shenanigans."

Sabrina nodded. "We're going to help rescue Granny Relda, whether Dad likes it or not."

"Right after you take a shower," Daphne said.

Sabrina sniffed her glop-covered shirt and gagged. "Right after I take a shower."

ABOUT THE AUTHOR

Michael Buckley is the *New York Times* bestselling author of the Sisters Grimm and NERDS series, *Kel Gilligan's Daredevil Stunt Show*, and the Undertow Trilogy. He has also written and developed television shows for many networks. Michael lives in Brooklyn, New York, with his wife, Alison; their son, Finn; and their dog, Friday.